Haven't we met someplace before?

Noah knelt down beside the girl he'd just hit with his car. "Are you hurt?" he asked. "Can you move?"

"Yes," she said. "I mean, no, I don't think I'm hurt. I can move." Then she opened her eyes. They were an astounding turquoise color, so bright they seemed lit from inside.

As soon as she looked at Noah, her mouth dropped open. "You're him," she breathed in an excited whisper. The girl threw her arms around Noah's neck. "I thought I'd never find you!" she cried. "I thought you were a dream."

"It's all right," Noah said awkwardly. "It'll all be okay."

The girl sniffed. She pulled back from him and looked up. Tears rolled down from her incredible turquoise eyes. "I've been looking for you for so long," she said, her voice raw with emotion. "I know you're the only one who can stop them."

"Who can I stop?" asked Noah, bewildered.

The girl pointed to the woods to the left of the road. "Them," she whispered.

Available from ARCHWAY Paperbacks

For orders other than by individual consumers, Pocket Books grants a discount on the purchase of **10 or more** copies of single titles for special markets or premium use. For further details, please write to the Vice-President of Special Markets, Pocket Books, 1633 Broadway, New York, NY 10019-6785, 8th Floor.

For information on how individual consumers can place orders, please write to Mail Order Department, Simon & Schuster Inc., 200 Old Tappan Road, Old Tappan, NJ 07675.

DARK
LIES

M.C. SUMNER

AN ARCHWAY PAPERBACK
Published by POCKET BOOKS
New York   London   Toronto   Sydney   Tokyo   Singapore

AN ARCHWAY PAPERBACK *Original*

 An Archway Paperback published by
POCKET BOOKS, a division of Simon & Schuster Inc.
1230 Avenue of the Americas, New York, NY 10020

Produced by Daniel Weiss Associates, Inc., New York

ISBN: 0-671-00242-2

First Archway Paperback printing February 1997

10 9 8 7 6 5 4 3 2 1

PROLOGUE

The dark man waited at the street corner for the last lights of the town to die.

Gradually the stores closed. The neon signs clicked off. Cars rolled past on their way home as the town emptied. Even then the dark man waited, hanging back, invisible in the shadows. He waited until the last car was gone and the town's single stoplight had begun to blink yellow and red. Waited for the clock on the old courthouse to chime midnight.

Then he moved.

In a larger city, there would have been more light. Someone there might have seen that the man's coat was old and tattered, that his hat was stained and beaten, and that his face was as dark as the night—darker. Within the camouflage of a shabby coat and a downturned hat brim, his features were a vague outline of obsidian blackness.

But this was not a large city, this was Stone Harbor. No one was there to see the dark man as he stalked up the empty street with a slow, halting gait. His feet, invisible below the flapping hem of his coat, scratched along the sidewalk with a sound

1

like steel wool rasping metal. The singular hiss echoed among the empty buildings and narrow alleys of the town.

When the dark man reached a small grocery store, he stopped in midstep. Turning slowly, he put a gloved hand against the front of the store and let it rest there for a long moment. He stood as still as a statue, his hand on the glass, holding his pose until a white mist of frost formed around his outstretched fingers. Then he stepped back from the door and raised his unseen face to the raw November wind, breathing in the air like a hound after a scent. The figure walked on.

At the front of the library he stopped again. Here the dark man pressed both hands against the door. Then he crushed his body, and finally even his face, against the library entranceway. Crystals of frost spread over wood and glass, silhouetting his black form. A long sigh escaped his unseen lips, a sound as dry as autumn leaves.

When he began to move again, he did so quickly. He was making other noises now. Grunting and panting with excitement, he turned east out of the business district, heading up a hill between old brick houses that had weathered more than a hundred harsh East Coast winters. Unable to restrain his eagerness, the dark man broke into a lopsided run for a few steps before slowing back to his hissing walk.

He paused at the next corner. There, one of the few streetlights still burning in Stone Harbor cast a yellow circle over the sidewalk and into the street. The dark figure reached his hand into the circle of light, then drew it back quickly, like a man sticking his toe into water and finding it far too cold. For a moment the black form was stone still.

Slowly the streetlight dimmed. Its yellow-white light faded to a fitful red glow. It buzzed and hummed like a bee caught in a jar. With a final snap, the light went out. A faint, deep noise rolled out over the dark street. It might have been laughter, but it was laughter as dark as the bottom of a well. The man moved on.

Finally his walk carried him through the older neighborhood and into an area of new construction. A hard wind blew in from the nearby ocean, sending his dirty, rat-gnawed coat flying out behind him. His feet hissed along, leaving their trail of frost.

A large two-story home dominated the area. The dark man lumbered up the sidewalk and leaned against the wide front door. Again frost rimmed his shape, but this time he rested against the wood for only a moment, then he went through the door. He didn't open it, he simply went *through*, entering the barrier of wood and metal as easily as if it were fog.

The dark man reappeared at the door, emerging slowly from the wood. He stepped out onto the sidewalk. The wind rose to a shriek as the man swept his hands over his sleeves, as if he were brushing away dust. Flakes of ice tumbled to the ground.

He lifted his invisible face to the wind. In the gloom that covered his features, there was the momentary gleam of something oily and smooth, like light shining against a black pearl.

Another form appeared in the shadows at the corner of the house. "This is the right house?" asked a voice that was quiet but commanding.

The dark man nodded slowly.

"And Templer is here?"

Another nod.

"Good. That's good." The second figure stepped forward. Dim light from a house down the street showed a slim silhouette against the night. "Come along," said the soft voice. "We have a lot of work to do."

The smaller form turned away and strolled off among the houses. The dark man stood in his circle of frost for a moment, then moved to follow. As his black form merged with the night, the sound of deep midnight laughter floated among the sleeping houses. Soon even that was lost in the voice of the wind.

ONE

Kathleen "Harley" Davisidaro stood at the end of a ragged point of land. A storm was coming. Below her the gray sea pounded against dark cliffs of weathered stone, crashing into foam with a noise like constant thunder. Harley leaned out over the water, her long black hair fluttering in the wind that blew up the rocks. Cold spray splashed against her face.

Harley leaned back from the edge. She shivered and closed the front of her jacket as tightly as she could. The jacket was a poor fit. She would have given a lot to have her old leather biking jacket. But the leather jacket was long gone. Most of Harley's clothing had been lost—along with her furniture, her books, her father, and anything that represented a normal life—when Unit 17 had abandoned the mysterious Tulley Hill Research Facility. Dee Janes and her family had given Harley a place to live. Dee had also passed along a few things to wear, but she was nowhere near Harley's size. Harley had purchased a few things on her own, but her supply of cash was small and dwindling fast.

The wind grew stronger, whipping Harley's hair against her face. She looked along the stony bluffs

5

and frowned. This is getting ridiculous, she thought. She looked down at her watch. It was already an hour past the time.

Ten more minutes, she decided. Ten more minutes, and I'm leaving.

Then she spotted movement around the curve of the harbor. Down on the stony beach, a figure was heading her way.

Harley crossed her arms and waited as the man climbed up the slope of broken rocks. The newcomer wore a tan trench coat over a well-cut black suit. On his head was an old-fashioned fedora with the brim turned down over his eyes. He stopped twenty feet away and stood with his hands shoved into the deep pockets of his coat.

"You're late," called Harley.

"I was detained," said the man. "I apologize, but it was an unavoidable delay."

Harley took a step toward him across the rough ground. "All right, Cain," she said. "I'm here. You're here. Now where's my father?"

A smile came to the man's long, sharp-chinned face. "I'm glad to see you decided to meet me, Ms. Davisidaro. And you came alone, as I instructed. Good. I was afraid that after our last encounter you might choose not to meet me again."

Harley shrugged. She didn't know how far she could trust this man. Cain had come to Harley and Noah claiming to be an FBI agent investigating

Unit 17. Harley now knew that was a lie. Still, Cain had helped them out of a tough situation—and possibly saved their lives.

"You already knew where I was," said Harley. "I got your note." She raised a hand to push her windblown hair back from her face. "I figured if you knew where to find me, the rest of them would, too."

Cain nodded. "That's healthy paranoia. But I hope you are incorrect." His gaze shifted past Harley, and he turned his head to look up the long, empty stretch of shoreline. "So far as I am aware, your location is not widely known. Even your identity is something of a secret."

"Unit Seventeen knows who I am," Harley replied.

"Yes," agreed Cain. "But there are others who do not. Just as there are some who know Mr. Templer's identity and some who do not. I have done my best to hide you both from prying eyes."

"Thanks," Harley said bitterly, "but don't do me any favors."

Cain shook his head. His sharp gaze returned to Harley. "It seems you don't appreciate my efforts on your behalf."

"How do I know you've *made* any efforts?" asked Harley. "You lied to me about being an FBI agent. You've been hiding the truth from me all along."

"I promise you," Cain replied, "I am as open as I can be."

"Then why didn't you want me to bring Noah along today?" Harley demanded. "He's just as involved in this thing as I am."

Instead of replying, the agent adjusted the position of his hat and once again looked around the empty expanse of bluffs and beach. If Harley didn't know better, she would have thought that the unflappable Agent Cain was actually nervous. Seeing him jumpy didn't do anything for Harley's own nerves. If he was afraid, there was probably a good reason.

From his pocket Cain drew a black pen, which he began to tumble back and forth among his long fingers. "This meeting is more dangerous than you realize. Adding Mr. Templer to the mix would have been . . . imprudent."

"Says who?" Nervousness made Harley's reply sound harsher than she had intended.

The pen stopped moving. "Me," replied Cain.

"I trust Noah a lot more than I trust you."

Cain suddenly shoved the pen back into his pocket, turned, and began to walk away.

"Where are you going?" called Harley. "We haven't talked about anything yet."

"Come with me," Cain said without looking back. "I want to show you something."

He led the way along the top of the bluff.

Harley followed, being careful not to step too close to the edge. Her sneakers were not the best kind of shoes for walking over rocks. The damp stones were slippery, and the water was a long, long way down.

After they had walked more than a hundred yards along the top of the cliff, Cain abruptly stopped. "There," he said, pointing at the ground.

Harley looked down. There was nothing to see but a small hole in the dark stone near the edge of the cliff. "What's in there?"

Cain again shoved his hands in the pockets of his coat. The man's lean features were tight, and with the coat flying out behind him he suddenly reminded Harley of a hawk. "Just wait," he said solemnly. "You'll see."

"See what?" asked Harley. When the agent didn't reply, she felt a tint of anger mixing with her nervousness. "This is all nonsense," she said through gritted teeth. "You got me out here today because you told me you knew something about my father. I only want my father back. Nothing else."

"Of course." Cain's voice was surprisingly gentle. For several seconds the man neither moved nor spoke. Finally he shifted his head slightly toward Harley. "I have information," he said softly.

"That's what you said in the note," replied

Harley. She folded her arms across her chest. She felt anxious to hear what Cain had to say, but she was trying not to get too excited, which probably would lead only to crushing disappointment. "Let's hear it."

"Before I can tell you what I know," said Cain, "I need you to perform a task."

"No," Harley answered immediately. "I knew it would be something like this. I knew you couldn't just tell me a simple piece of information." She shook her head sharply. "I'm not doing anything for you until I know where to find my father."

Cain looked at her, his deep-set eyes almost lost in the shadow of his hat. "This is a job that must be done." he told her. "If you aren't willing, then we have nothing further to discuss."

Harley clenched her fists. She wanted to scream. She wanted to knock Cain down and kick him until he told her what she wanted to know. But Harley swallowed her anger. "This is blackmail," she said in a cold voice.

"Call it what you will," said Cain with a shrug. His expression was flat, displaying no more emotion than if he were talking about the price of milk. "I'll reveal my information only if you'll agree to complete this task."

Harley bit her lip. Cain was the one remaining link that might lead to her father. Harley's mother had died when Harley was only five, leaving her father to raise her on his own. She had a little-seen aunt on the other side of the country, but Harley's father had been her only real family. In the three weeks since his disappearance, Harley hadn't turned up a single clue about where her father had gone. Dee Janes's father was the local police chief, and he had been checking every available source, but nothing had turned up. Harley hadn't learned the first thing about where her father was or about the mysterious Unit 17 that had taken him. If Harley didn't deal with Cain, she might never find him again.

"All right," she agreed. "What do you want me to do?"

Cain smiled again. He reached into the folds of his coat and produced a pale blue envelope. "You'll find directions inside," he said.

Harley stepped over to him and took the envelope from his hand. It was thick, packed with papers. She pulled out the top sheet and found herself looking at a map of city streets. "New York?" She looked up, puzzled. "I've never been to New York."

Cain turned and stared out over the waves. "Unit Seventeen has established a presence in the city," he said. "We need to know what they're planning."

Harley looked at the stack of papers and slowly

shook her head. "I can't go that far away from Stone Harbor. Unit Seventeen has erased my identity from all the government records. They've put together a fake identity that's wanted by the police. My face is on posters in every post office in the country."

"Then maybe you should change your face," suggested Cain. He stretched out his hand and tapped the envelope. "In the meantime, take a look at what else is inside."

Harley reached in and drew out another sheet. When she saw what was printed on the page, she blinked in surprise. "It's somebody's birth certificate."

Cain took the piece of paper from her hands. "It's *your* birth certificate, Kathleen Elise *Vincent.*" He glanced at the paper, nodded, and handed it back. "Also in the envelope you'll find a driver's license, a social security card, and a brief summary to help you learn a few relevant details of Ms. Vincent's life. High-school transcript. Parents. The name of your third-grade teacher." Cain gave a satisfied smile. "All the little details that make a person real."

Harley dug into the envelope and came out with a plastic-coated driver's license. To her surprise, the card didn't look new. The edges were tattered and the plastic was yellowed, as though the card had been in someone's pocket for at least a year. There was a smiling face in the corner.

"It's me," Harley said in wonder.

"Of course it is." He pointed at the birth certificate in Harley's hand. "In fact, if someone checks the little footprints on this certificate, they'll find they're a match. They can check anything about Kathy Vincent that they like. Everything is in place."

Harley shoved the birth certificate back in the envelope and ran a finger over the smooth surface of the driver's license. "My hair's short in this picture."

"Just a suggestion," replied Cain. "Your hair is one of your most distinctive features. Change it, and you'll go a long way toward changing your appearance."

Unconsciously Harley twisted a lock of hair between her fingers. She had kept her thick black hair long and straight for as long as she could remember. It was often a pain to take care of it, but she had never really thought about changing the style. "You seem awfully good at this false-identity business," she told Cain.

The agent turned away again, watching the waves roll toward the shore. "It is a skill that I have practiced many times. A most *necessary* skill. By the way, if you look in the bottom of that envelope, I believe you'll find a considerable sum of cash—two thousand dollars."

Harley felt her heart skip a beat. "Two thousand dollars?" She pulled open the mouth of the envelope and saw a dark green bundle of bills. Ever since her father had disappeared, Harley had been getting along on handouts from Dee and her family. Two thousand dollars seemed like a lot more money than it had when her father was bringing home a paycheck every week.

"The money should cover any expenses you encounter," said Cain. "Don't spend it all in one place."

"I won't." Harley looked up and studied the man's sharp-chinned profile. "Who are you?" she asked. "Who do you really work for?"

Instead of answering, Cain spun around and clamped his big hands on Harley's shoulders. "Stand very still."

Fear swept over Harley. "What—?"

"Shhh," hissed Cain. *"Listen."*

At first Harley heard nothing. Then she noticed a low moaning, a note so deep she felt it more with her stomach than her ears. The sound grew rapidly louder, and as it swelled in volume it also rose in pitch. It became a bass howl. Then a steamship whistle. Then an overwhelming shriek.

From the dark hole in the stone a column of water shot into the air. It rose twenty feet above the hole, spouting like a geyser.

Harley tried to step back, but Cain's grip was

like an iron clamp. He held her still while the fountaining water reached a peak, soaring over their heads. Then, almost as suddenly as it had started, it disappeared. The column of water splashed against the stones. The shriek abruptly stopped. The opening in the rocks was again only a dark hole.

Cain relaxed his grip on Harley's shoulders. "There," he said. "You see?"

Harley nodded, her heart pounding in her ears. "What was that? Another high-tech trick?"

The agent smiled again, and for the first time Harley thought his expression was almost compassionate. "I assure you," he said, "that what you just witnessed was a purely natural phenomenon." Cain leaned out over the edge of the cliff and pointed toward the water. "There's a small sea cave down there that connects to this opening. Most of the time nothing happens. But on rare days, when a storm is at hand and the waves are just right, you get a spectacular result."

"I'll say," agreed Harley. "And this is what you wanted me to see?"

Cain nodded. "Yes." He leaned down, and his angular face was cast in shadow. "Sometimes the world is just like this waterspout. Everything goes along quietly for a very long time. Everything stays in balance. But then a storm draws close." He paused again to stare out over the water.

"Is a storm coming now?" asked Harley.

"Yes," whispered Cain.

"What kind of storm?"

"Asymmetry," Cain replied. "An imbalance that leads to chaos."

He stopped again, and Harley shivered in the cold wind. "What—" she began.

Cain held up a finger, silencing her. "New powers are emerging," he said. "Powers that could erase the fragile order that has held for so long." He turned and looked at her, his gray eyes suddenly fierce. "You and Noah are making waves, Harley. We have to be careful, very careful, or those waves could drown us all."

With that, he spun around and began to walk quickly away.

"Wait!" Harley called. She hurried after him. "What about my father?"

The agent stopped. Slowly he reached into his coat and drew out another envelope. "Are you going to do as I ask?" he demanded. "Are you prepared to complete the task for which you've been chosen?"

The way he asked his questions made Harley feel strange. There was suddenly a singsong quality in Cain's voice, as if the words were part of some ancient chant. "Yeah," said Harley. "At least, I'll try."

Cain turned and shoved the second envelope

into her hands. "Take care how you use this," he said. "Not everything is what it seems. And whatever you do, don't tell Noah what I've said or what I've given you. He has his own test to face."

Harley unfolded the top of the envelope and reached in. Her fingers closed on something small and hard. She pulled it out and found herself looking at one of her father's journals. "I *knew* you were the one who took this," she said under her breath. "Why did you—"

She looked up and discovered that she was talking to herself. She turned around, searching in all directions. Though she could see for miles along the bare curve of the shore, there was no sign of Cain.

Harley shivered again, this time not just from the cold. Then she pulled her thin jacket closed and hurried away.

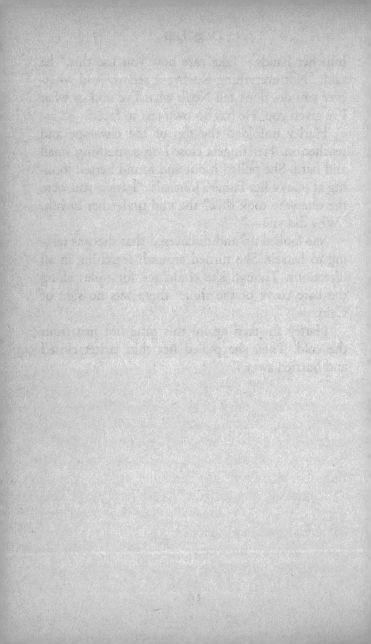

T W O

"But it has to be there!"

Noah Templer tore the X-ray plate from the hands of the doctor and studied the stark black-and-white image. He was certainly no expert, but Noah could see the curve of his jawbone, the vertebrae of his neck, and the bones of his shoulder. Softer tissue had left blurry gray streaks on the X ray. Nowhere was there any sign of the thing he had expected to see below his shoulder blade.

"It has to be there," Noah said again, but this time his voice was quiet and uncertain. He held the sheet up to the light and squinted.

Dr. Worthington took the plate back and slid it into a folder. "I'm sorry," she said. "Well, actually, I'm not sorry. I'm quite glad. And you should be, as well. This X ray indicates absolutely nothing unusual in your neck or shoulder." She closed the folder. "I'm not sure what caused you to believe there ever was something there."

"Someone showed me," Noah said. "He held up a . . . a . . . a *something*, and it showed that something was in my shoulder."

The doctor frowned. "Of course. Someone showed you something with a something." She shook her head. "I don't know how I let you talk me into doing this X ray, but I hope that the results prove to you that there's nothing there. Now if you'll excuse me, I have other work to do." She stuck the folder under her arm and left the room.

Noah sat down on the edge of the examining table. It had been Ian Cain who told him about the device hidden in the flesh of his shoulder. Over a period of only a few days, people had tried to kill Noah three times. Cain said they had used the device under Noah's skin to locate him. But the X ray showed no device. It showed nothing at all.

Maybe Cain had lied. Or maybe . . . maybe the problem was the doctor.

Noah looked toward the door. He already knew that at least three people in town had been involved with Legion and Unit 17. There could always be more. If the doctor was working for Legion, then of course she would say there was nothing in Noah's shoulder. Legion had put it there in the first place.

As Noah thought about Legion, the room around him seemed to undergo a subtle transformation. The lights dimmed, leaving the corners of the room in darkness. The examining table changed from padded vinyl into a slab of cold, bare metal. From out of the darkness emerged small, pale forms with huge midnight black eyes. A murmur of strange voices rose in his ears.

Noah shook his head sharply. The vision vanished in a flash, leaving the doctor's office just as it had been. Noah rubbed his eyes. The dreams were not as frequent as they had been in the three previous weeks, but they had not gone away completely. The nightmares were still there, ready to pull him down into the darkness if he wasn't careful.

A knock at the door made Noah jump. "Who is it?" he blurted out.

The door opened, and Harley Davisidaro stuck her head inside. "Are you decent?"

Noah licked his lips and tried to work up a welcoming smile. "I was only getting an X ray. You don't get have to get undressed for that."

Harley slipped into the room and closed the door behind her. "You can never tell," she said. "Doctors are always in a hurry to make you take your clothes off."

"Maybe you should be a little more suspicious of doctors," Noah suggested. He said it as a joke, but there was still a real concern in his mind.

"Maybe so," Harley replied. She smiled uncertainly.

Noah was glad to see that he could still get Harley to smile, even just a little. Since her father had disappeared, there hadn't been much that could cheer Harley up. She had no family in Stone Harbor, and only a few friends. If it weren't for Noah, and for Dee Janes, Harley would have been alone.

"So, when are they taking out the thing?" asked Harley.

"What thing?"

"The thing in your shoulder." Harley walked around the room, running her finger over plastic-coated anatomy charts. "Did they take it out yet? Did they give it to you?"

Noah looked down at the floor. "They couldn't find anything."

"But Cain said it was there."

"I know." Noah ran his hand along the skin at the bottom of his shoulder blade, where Cain had said the device was hidden. "I'm not sure how much we can trust Cain."

"I hope we can trust him," Harley muttered.

"What?"

Harley shook her head. "Never mind." She sat down on the edge of the table beside Noah, her leg brushing against his. "You know," she said, "just because they didn't find anything, that doesn't mean it's not there."

"I guess," Noah mumbled.

"Sure," said Harley. "You saw all the equipment inside that Unit Seventeen base. They have technologies that no one has ever heard about. If Legion has things like that, then who knows? They could make something invisible to

X rays." She shrugged. "At least Cain said he changed the frequency on it so that Legion can't use it anymore."

Noah nodded. "That's what he said. But I hate the thought of that thing being inside of me. What if Legion *can* still tap into it? How can I live knowing they could find me anytime they want me?"

Harley reached up and ran her fingers lightly over the skin on Noah's shoulder. "Just because they didn't find it," she repeated softly, "that doesn't mean it's not there."

"Can you feel anything?" Noah asked. He lowered his head and looked down at the floor to give Harley better access to his back.

"No. No, not really." Harley's fingers pushed into Noah's muscles. "But that doesn't mean anything, either. There are other tests they can do. Ultrasounds. CAT scans. Or maybe even an MRI."

Noah frowned. "If they can hide this thing from X rays, then who knows if it'll show up on anything else?"

"Cain found it with that rod he was using." Harley brushed her slender fingers over the fine hairs on the back of Noah's neck. "If it's real, there has to be some test that will find it."

"Yeah, but I'm not sure if the doctor will run any of those tests." Noah raised his head. He was about to say something more, but at that point he turned to face Harley.

He had been so distracted by the X-ray business that he hadn't even really looked at her. Now her dark eyes were right there in front of him. Her long hair spilled down to brush across Noah's arm. He could feel the warmth of her in the cold examining room. He was suddenly very aware of Harley's hand on his neck.

Noah swallowed hard. He wasn't sure what he should do. He had an urge to grab Harley right then and there and kiss her. If things hadn't been so crazy, they might have had a completely different relationship. Maybe they still would.

He reached up and put his hand over hers. "Maybe I should get back to school now," he suggested softly. "Afternoon classes are going to start any minute now."

A series of emotions crossed Harley's face. Her full lips pressed together. "Sure," she said. She sounded disappointed.

Noah gave her hand a squeeze before letting go. "I'll be by later to help you get your stuff."

Harley frowned. "Are you sure this move is a good idea?"

"You were the one who first suggested it," said Noah. "You said you were worried about what might happen to Dee and her family if Unit Seventeen came after you."

"I know," Harley replied. She looked away, and for the second time Noah had the impression that Harley was hiding something.

"You don't have to move," he said.

Harley shook her head. "No. As long as you're sure this place will be okay."

"It'll be fine," Noah assured her. "You'll see. My parents bought this little cabin way back before they had money." He put an oh-so-upper-class accent into his voice. "It's *ever* so unfashionable. Mummy and Daddy wouldn't *dream* of going there now." Noah let his voice return to normal. "Seriously, I don't think anybody's used this place in years. I've paid cash to get the electricity working again. It'll be a perfect hiding place."

The door suddenly opened, and Dr. Worthington stepped into the room. She seemed surprised to see Noah. "Are you still here, Mr. Templer? We need to get this room ready for another patient."

Noah pushed himself off the table and stood up straight. "We were just leaving," he said.

The doctor stood by the door until Noah and Harley had left the room. Then she shut the door with a click.

Noah stopped in the hallway and looked over his shoulder at the closed door. He wondered again if Dr. Worthington was involved. She had been his doctor for as long as he could remember. But that didn't mean anything.

Josh McQuinn had been his friend all his life, but Josh had turned out to be watching Noah for the group called Legion. Noah's girlfriend, Caroline, had been with Unit 17. Even the school track coach had been an agent.

Legion and Unit 17 seemed to be everywhere. Anybody could be an agent for one of these shadowy, powerful organizations. *Anybody.*

Someone touched Noah's arm. He jumped and spun around. His hands clenched into fists.

"What's wrong?" Harley asked. She took a step backward, looking down at Noah's hands.

Noah shook his head. "Nothing. Nothing's wrong." He walked quickly to the door of the medical building and stepped outside.

Harley came out a moment later. "You sure you're okay?"

"I'm fine," he said, working up a smile. "I think I really should get to school. You need a ride over to Dee's?"

"I've got my Sportster," said Harley. She pointed across the parking lot at the shiny black-and-chrome motorcycle.

"All right then." Noah hesitated. He felt as though there should be more. But he wasn't sure what.

Harley solved the problem. She stepped over to

Noah, stood on tiptoe, and planted a quick kiss on his cheek.

"Be careful," she whispered in his ear.

Before Noah could reply, Harley stepped away and hurried to her bike. Noah stood in the parking lot and watched as Harley pulled on her helmet and sped away. Then he went to his own Mustang and headed toward school.

He wished Harley were coming with him. But Harley had decided that it was too dangerous. Coach Rocklin, the track coach, had been a Unit 17 agent planted at the school to watch Harley. Rocklin was gone, but that didn't mean there wasn't another agent ready to take her place. Harley didn't want Unit 17 tracking her back to Dee's house.

Besides, Harley's identity had been stolen—all her school records had been wiped clean. Even if she convinced the people at Stone Harbor High School to let her attend again, there were no transcripts available from her other schools to replace the missing ones. Unless everything was fixed, Harley would never be able to graduate from high school.

For Noah there was less risk in going to school. He was still living in his own house. He still had his own name. If someone was trying to find him, going to class wasn't going to make much difference.

Noah suddenly felt a wave of dizziness, followed by an overwhelming feeling that someone was watching him. He glanced up into his rearview mirror just in time to see a black car pull onto the road. Instantly he stepped on the gas and shot right past the high school. He took a quick right into a narrow road, then a left. Then another right.

On a small tree-lined back street Noah slowed and glanced behind him. Ten seconds went by with no sign of the dark car. Twenty.

Noah let out a deep breath. A dark sedan had tried to run him down three weeks earlier. Another one had crashed into a car that Harley and Noah were riding in, pushing them off the road. But this time nothing had happened.

Not too long ago, Noah would have assumed this was a false alarm. After all, not every black car could be filled with sinister agents. Now he wasn't so sure. It was safer to believe that everyone was an enemy and then sort them out later.

He waited on the street for another five minutes. A white-haired woman emerged from a small white house down the block and carried a plastic sack out to the street. Noah watched her carefully in his rearview mirror. She looked like an old woman taking out the trash. But she could also be an agent. Anyone could be. Noah started the car and drove slowly away. He kept his eyes on the mirror, watching the old woman.

There was a thump from the front of the car. Noah looked down just in time to see a small figure in dark clothing bounce away from the front bumper and fall to the ground.

Icy fear dropped over Noah. He had been paying so much attention to the old woman that he had *hit* someone. He smashed on the brakes and scrambled out of the car.

As he ran around the front of the Mustang, Noah dreaded what he might find. What he saw as the passenger side came into view only confirmed his fears.

A girl lay stretched out on the ground beside the car. Her arms were spread across the gravel at the side of the road. Her legs trailed into a patch of weeds.

She was small, and Noah's first, horrified thought was that he had struck a child. But as he bent down beside the girl, he realized that she was older, closer to his own age.

Noah touched her lightly on her back. "I'm so sorry," he said. "I didn't see you."

To Noah's relief, the girl moaned and turned over. She was thin, with fine, delicate features and long red hair. Dirt was streaked across her cheeks, and there were bits of twigs and leaves caught in her hair. Despite the cold weather, she wore a dark sleeveless shirt that exposed pale shoulders and slender arms.

Moving carefully, Noah knelt down beside her. "Are you hurt?" he asked. "Can you move?"

The girl nodded. "Yes," she said. "I mean, no, I don't think I'm hurt. I can move." There was a warm southern accent in her voice that immediately established she wasn't a native of Stone Harbor. Then she opened her eyes. They were an

29

astounding turquoise color, so bright they seemed lit from inside.

As soon as she looked at Noah, her mouth dropped open. "You're him," she breathed in an excited whisper.

Noah blinked in surprise. "What?"

The girl sat up, then threw her arms around Noah's neck. She buried her face against his chest. Her slender back heaved with her sobs. "I thought I'd never find you," she cried. "I thought you were a dream."

Noah was frozen for a moment. Then he put his hands against the girl's back and held her carefully. "It's all right," he said. "It'll all be okay."

The girl sniffed. She pulled back from him and looked up. Tears rolled down from her incredible turquoise eyes. "I've been looking for you for so long," she said as her voice grew raw with emotion and her accent became stronger.

"For me?"

The girl nodded. "I know you're the only one who can help me. You're the only one who can stop them."

"Help how?" asked Noah, bewildered. "Who can I stop?"

The girl's eyes shifted left and right. She raised a finger and pointed to the woods to the left of the road. "Them," she whispered.

Noah turned his head and saw shafts of red light

slipping between the trees. Goose bumps broke out over his skin. He didn't have to see what was causing the light to know what was coming through the woods. He had seen a light like that before.

He bit his lip and turned back to the girl. "Can you get up?"

She nodded and stretched up her hands. "I can if you'll help me."

Noah grabbed the girl's hands and pulled her up as gently as he could. Holding her in the crook of one arm, he used the other hand to tug open the passenger door on the Mustang and help her inside. Just as he was closing the door, a sphere of light emerged from the woods.

It was smaller than the one Noah had seen before, no bigger than a softball, but it was bright, almost too bright to look at. It was so red, it seemed like the essence of the color—a ball of blazing, boiling crimson. The sphere slipped out to the edge of the woods and hovered there as if it was frightened of the sunlight beyond.

Noah had seen a sphere like that twice previously. Both times it had appeared near agents of Legion or Unit 17. Keeping his eye on the sphere, Noah slid around the car. He felt the familiar sensation of dancing ants moving over all his exposed skin. The air was filled with a sharp bite of ozone. Noah backed into the car and softly shut his door.

He looked to his right. The girl was slumped in her seat with her head tipped over to the side. Her extraordinary eyes were closed.

Noah took her by the wrist. "Are you all right?" he asked.

The girl didn't move. She seemed to be unconscious. Or maybe worse.

Noah found his breath coming in deep gulps. He wasn't sure what he should do. Clearly the girl needed help. Stone Harbor was too small to have a real hospital. He could take the girl to the medical center. But if Dr. Worthington really was involved, taking the girl to the medical center would be the same as delivering her right into the hands of Legion.

Noah looked back toward the woods. The ball of light hovered right outside his window, only inches away from his face. Noah let out his breath in a wordless shout. Without thinking, he threw the car into gear and stomped on the gas. Gravel fountained out behind the tires as the car fishtailed down the narrow lane.

A glance in the mirror showed the sphere of light still floating over the middle of the road. It didn't seem to be following. But Noah was ten miles away before he dared slow down.

Harley pulled up the blinds and peered out the window for the fifth time in the past hour. "He's late," she said. "Something's wrong."

Dee Janes sat down on the end of the bed. She took off her glasses and rubbed her eyes. "He's only ten minutes late. I wouldn't start worrying yet."

"I would," Harley said. "After everything that's happened, I don't do much *but* worry." She let the blinds fall over the window and turned to face Dee. "If I *stop* worrying, then we're in real trouble."

"Nothing's happened since the base closed," Dee reminded her. "I know you're worried about your dad, but you and Noah have to relax. If you keep thinking someone's about to shoot you all the time, you're both going . . ." Dee waved her hands around, looking for the right words. A look of painful frustration crossed her round face. "I don't know," she said. "You're just going to explode, or just plain go nuts."

"I'm already there," Harley muttered under her breath.

"What?"

"Never mind."

Dee scooted back to the end of the bed and leaned against the wall. Her oversized shirt stretched all the way down to her knees. "Yeah, well . . . all this paranoid stuff only proves you're not ready to move out."

Harley shook her head. "You don't understand. I have to move."

"I think you should stay here." Dee folded her arms behind her head and leaned back, her auburn hair draping over her arms. "You move to some little shack out in the middle of nowhere, and, well . . ." She shrugged. "Who knows how crazy you might get without my practical, intelligent example?"

Despite herself, Harley laughed for a moment. "This is serious," she said once she had regained her composure. "Every day I stay here is putting your family at risk."

"See, that's another sign of creeping paranoia," Dee argued. "No one has threatened us. No one even knows you're here."

"Someone does," said Harley.

"Who?"

Harley bit her lip. She had a decision to make, and it wasn't an easy one. Should she trust Dee? "There's something I want to tell you," she said carefully. "Something I don't want even Noah to hear."

Dee reached up with one finger and settled her glasses back on her nose. Through the heavy lenses her green eyes were huge and bright. "You're going to tell me a secret that *Noah* doesn't know?" She leaned forward on the bed. "Cool!"

Harley winced. "I'll tell you only if you promise to stop yelling about it."

"I'll stop," said Dee. She drew her hand over her face as if sealing her lips. "See? I can be really, really quiet," she said in a soft whisper.

"I hope so." Harley went to the bedroom door and made sure no one was standing in the hall. Then she shut the door firmly. "I wish I *could* tell Noah about this, but I made a promise not to."

"Who did you promise?" asked Dee.

Harley hesitated a moment. "Cain."

Dee sat still for a moment, then opened her eyes even wider. Magnified by the glasses, they seemed as large as golf balls. "That's the guy who told you he was some kind of secret agent, right?"

"Yeah," Harley answered with a nod. "And I guess he really *is* a secret agent. I just don't know who he's an agent *for.*"

"When did you talk to this Cain guy?" asked Dee.

"Yesterday."

"Yesterday! How did—" Dee caught herself in midshout. "Sorry," she said. "I'll stay quiet. But how . . . I mean, *where* did you see this Cain?"

Harley reached into the pocket of her jeans and pulled out a small strip of paper that was rolled up like a tiny scroll. "Yesterday morning I went down to check on my bike, and I found this sitting on the seat."

Dee took the paper from Harley's fingers and stretched it out between her hands. "'I have information concerning your father,'" she read. "'Meet on shore one-point-five miles north of pier. Six P.M. Tell no one. Come alone. Cain.'" Dee looked up from the paper. "Wow. And you actually went?"

Harley nodded. "I went." She walked across the room and dropped into a chair. "I talked to Cain last night."

"So? What did he say? Does he really know where your dad is?"

"He says he does." Harley shrugged. "I don't know. He wants me to do something for him."

"What?"

Harley quickly recounted her conversation with the mysterious agent. "He says I can't tell Noah anything," she finished. "But I had to tell someone. Just in case."

"In case of what?" asked Dee.

"In case I don't come back," Harley replied softly. She fought back a shiver. She had been thinking about the errand's dangers all day, but saying the words made her feel strange, as though admitting she could die might make it come true.

Dee tossed Cain's note on the bed. "You mean

you're going to do what Cain said?" She shook her head. "That's crazy. You can't really go all the way to New York."

Harley leaned forward, putting her elbows on her knees and holding her hair back from her face with both hands. "I have to go," she said with a confidence she didn't really feel. "It's the only way I have of finding out about my dad."

For long seconds there was nothing but silence in the room. Then the bedsprings squealed as Dee jumped to her feet. "Fine," she declared. "I'm coming with you."

"You can't do that," Harley told her.

"Sure I can." Dee paced around the room. "I'll tell my parents that I'm going out to stay with you for a few days. You know, help you get settled in. Then the two of us can sneak off to New York and be back before anyone even notices."

"No," Harley said firmly. "Cain told me I had to go alone." She moved her hands and let her hair fall across her face. "I shouldn't have said anything."

"I'm coming with you," Dee insisted. "You're going to need—"

There was a sudden rap on the bedroom door. "Harley? Dee? Are you guys in there?" called Noah's voice from the hallway.

Harley looked up quickly. "Don't say anything about this," she whispered fiercely. "Not a word."

Dee nodded. "All right." She went to the bedroom door and opened it. "Come on in. I think Harley's all packed for the road."

"That's great," said Noah. But instead of waiting for Harley to come out, he stepped into the room and shut the door behind him.

Harley pushed her hair out of her face and stared at Noah. There was something different about him, a kind of nervous energy she hadn't seen since they broke into the Unit 17 base where her father had disappeared. "What's up?" she asked.

Noah licked his lips. "I've found another," he said.

"Another what?" Harley asked with a frown.

Noah walked across the room and crouched down in front of her. "Another one like me," he said. "Someone who's been experimented on by Legion."

Harley looked at Noah's flushed face. It was obvious he was excited, but she didn't know how she felt about this sudden piece of information. "Are you sure?" she asked.

He nodded. "I'm sure. Everything matches up. The room, the aliens—everything I remember in my dreams. She's even been chased by one of the light spheres."

"She?" Dee asked. "It's a woman?"

Noah looked around at Dee and nodded. "Yes.

Or a girl. I mean, she's our age. Or maybe a little younger." He shrugged. "I didn't ask."

Harley felt an odd tingle in her stomach. It wasn't really fear. At least, not yet. But she was nervous. Ever since this thing had started, it had been just Harley and Noah. They had shared some of their secrets with Dee and her family, but all the real action had been just between the two of them. The idea of someone else—of another girl—being involved disturbed Harley in a way she couldn't name.

"Where did you meet this girl?" she asked. "Did you find her on the Internet?"

Noah shook his head. "No," he said. "She's here! She's right here in Stone Harbor."

"Someone else from town is involved in all this?" said Dee. "Someone we know?"

"No." Noah frowned. He shifted his weight from foot to foot—he was obviously having trouble containing his excitement. "Come on," he said to Harley. "Let's get all your stuff and get going. I've got her stashed out at the cabin. You can meet her when we get there."

The idea of meeting this mysterious girl didn't appeal to Harley, especially when she was still trying to work out how she was going to follow Cain's instructions. But she picked up the box containing her meager belongings and carried it down to Noah's car.

Dee hopped into the Mustang with Noah, while Harley followed behind on her motorcycle. The miniature convoy rolled out of Stone Harbor and into the wooded hills south of town. Off to the left, Harley caught occasional glimpses of the sea, but as the road wound back into the hills, those glimpses became fewer and farther between. Dark woods pressed in on the sides of the road.

Ten miles out of town, Noah turned off onto a gravel path. Harley drove carefully, downshifting through the gears. She steered around potholes and loose rocks as she guided the big Sportster down a steep incline and around a series of tight turns. Even though Harley avoided the worst bumps, the road was still a rough ride. Ahead of her, Noah's Mustang raised a plume of dust from the dry gravel, making the trip doubly unpleasant.

Water appeared ahead. At first Harley thought they had reached another arm of the sea, but this water was smooth, greenish, and calm. A lake. Clusters of cabins and small houses lined the banks. Floating docks jutted out into the water, but there were few boats to be seen. From the shuttered windows and leaf-littered yards, it was obvious that these were summer places, most of them probably owned by people who lived hundreds of miles away. Some were so broken-down that it was clear they had been abandoned.

Noah drove on past the main group of cabins, crossed a small bridge over the lake, then pulled off to the side of the road. Even before Harley managed to park her bike, Noah was out of the car.

"Come on," he called as Harley pulled in behind the Mustang. He reached into the back of the car and brought out the box of Harley's things. "Let's go."

"Go where?" asked Harley. She pulled off her helmet and looked around. From where they were standing, she couldn't see a single building.

Noah walked over to the edge of the woods. "The cabin's down here," he called. Then he stepped into the heavy forest and disappeared.

Dee and Harley crunched across the gravel to the place where Noah had vanished. Between the densely spaced trunks of pine and ash, a narrow trail was outlined by tan stones.

"Very inviting," Dee said sarcastically as she stared into the shaded forest. "You think you'll have an outhouse down there, or are you just expected to find a nice private bush?"

"I'm sure it'll be fine," said Harley.

Dee nodded. "Yeah. It looks like a great place to find guys wearing hockey masks and carrying chain saws."

"It's just the woods," Harley replied calmly.

"Let's go." She started down the path, but Dee took her by the arm.

"Hold on a sec." Dee leaned in closer and dropped her voice to a whisper. "What do you think about this girl Noah's found?"

Harley shrugged. "How can I know what I think about her? I haven't even met her."

"You haven't met *her,*" Dee shot back, "but you've seen *him.*" She looked off down the path and shook her head. "I've never seen anyone so smitten so fast."

"Noah's not smitten," Harley said firmly. "He's just excited to find someone else who's been through some of the same things he has. I'm sure he hopes to find out more information."

Dee nodded. "Sure," she said, her voice dripping with sarcasm. "Guys drool like that all the time at the idea of *information.*" She rolled her eyes. "Come on. This girl has hit Noah like a train. What are you going to do about it?"

Harley shook her head. "Why should I do anything about it? Noah and I are just friends. More like business partners."

She pulled free of Dee and started down the path in the woods. As she walked she tried to tell herself that there really *was* nothing between her and Noah—nothing but a lot of secrets they couldn't share with anyone else. Except now Noah had found someone new to trust.

The path led down a slope into a maze of huge

sandstone boulders that were grouped together, forming a network of miniature canyons. Harley picked her way among the stones with Dee following close behind. In one spot the path ran straight through a crack in a towering mass of rock. In another place the trail entered a field of haystack boulders overgrown by moss and lichens. The woods were cool, green, and quiet. If it hadn't been for the stones set into the ground, Harley knew, it would be easy to get lost.

Finally the roof of a cabin appeared on the slope below. The cabin was small, with walls made from split logs turned and varnished a deep red-gold. Along one side of the building a small stream, gleaming like gold in the afternoon sun, tumbled over rocks and splashed down to the edge of the lake. The whole place was altogether beautiful, and one hundred percent nicer than anything Harley had expected.

On the tiny porch at the front of the cabin, Noah stood waiting with a broad smile on his face. Next to him stood a petite girl with red hair and bright blue-green eyes.

"Harley," Noah said, "I'd like you to meet Billie."

"Nice to meet you," said Harley. She stepped forward and took the girl's pale fingers in her own. She tried to keep a smile on her face, but with every passing second Harley was becoming more certain of the real name for the uncomfortable feeling down in her gut.

It was called jealousy.

FOUR

Noah sat cross-legged on the floor in front of the fireplace. On his left was Harley. On his right was Dee. A fire burned at their backs, casting flickering red-and-black shadows across the room.

In front of them sat Billie.

"So much of what happened to me is a blur," said the red-haired girl. She huddled in an old chair, a blanket draped over her slender shoulders. "I was there for so long, I can barely remember a time before I was a prisoner."

Harley spoke up. "Where are you from?"

"Georgia," said Billie. Then she frowned. "I know it was a small town. Near a city, I think." She ran one hand over her pale face. "Isn't it terrible? I can remember what things looked like. I can remember my house, and my parents, and my school. But the names of things have all run together." Her red lips trembled, and again her eyes brimmed with tears. "I'm not even sure about *my* name."

"That's all right," Noah said quickly. "It'll come back to you. Now that you've gotten away, you'll start to remember. Just like I've been remembering what they did to me."

Billie nodded and dabbed at her eyes. "I hope so. But just about all I *can* remember is what they did to me." She swallowed, and her voice took on a raw edge. "I remember too much about that."

"Do you have any idea where you were a prisoner?" asked Harley.

"A dark place," Billie replied. "There was a room where they kept me. A room with no light. And then the room with the table." She stopped for a moment, then pulled in a deep breath. "Anyway, I don't think it was too far away from here. At least, I wasn't in the van for very long."

Her description of the room matched the place Noah had talked about seeing in his nightmarish dreams, but he certainly didn't remember anything about a van. "Why were you in the van?" he asked.

Billie shrugged. "I'm not really sure. The tall ones said they were going to move me to a new place."

Noah frowned in puzzlement. "The tall ones?"

"That's what I called them," said Billie. She turned and faced the shadowed corner of the cabin's single main room. "The people that held me—that is, the *things* that held me—came in three kinds. Some of them looked just like people, but I don't think they were people." She shivered violently. "They just didn't feel right."

"There was a person in my dreams, too," Noah agreed. "But when I saw that person get shot—in real life—he sure didn't die like a normal person."

"Those were the ones I called the tall ones. Then there were the dark ones. Those were shaped like people, but they were nothing *but* shapes. Like shadows come to life."

There had been plenty of darkness in the dreams, but Noah didn't remember any of it being alive. He thought hard, but after a moment he shook his head. "I don't remember anything like that."

"The last kind was the aliens," Billie continued. "They were small, with white skin and big dark eyes."

"Yes," said Noah excitedly. Her description of the aliens exactly matched how he remembered them from his dreams.

Billie paused. In the fireplace a piece of wood shifted, giving birth to sparks that trailed out into the dimly lit room. "The aliens watched me," she whispered. "They watched me all the time. But it was the tall ones who did most of the hurting."

"You mean they operated on you," Noah clarified. He touched his shoulder. "They operated on me, too. They put something under the skin at the top of my shoulder blade."

"I guess you could say they operated on me." Billie shivered. She tugged on the blanket, pulling it tight around herself. "But if it was for any reason, I don't know. Mostly they just hurt me. They cut me. Sometimes they cut me a little. Sometimes a lot." She raised her right hand and ran her fingers slowly along her left palm. "They sliced the skin on my arms. Once they even cut my arm off at the elbow."

Noah jolted in surprise. "They did *what?*"

Harley shook her head. "That's impossible," she said bluntly. "No one can grow back an arm."

"You think I don't know that?" Billie replied. She shivered again. "But they really did cut my arm off. I saw them do it. And it *hurt.*" She looked around at Noah, her eyes almost orange in the firelight. Then she squeezed her eyes shut tightly. "It hurt more than I thought anything *could* hurt. I can still see just how it looked. My arm lying over on a table, the skin going gray and all the blood pouring into the drains at the side of the table."

Noah winced at the thought. He could imagine the scene all too well: the black shadows of the room, the white faces of the aliens, the gleaming metal table, the bright red blood.

With her eyes still closed, Billie held up her small hand and flexed her fingers. "I cried myself to sleep that night with nothing but a stump where my arm should have been. But when I woke up in the morning, my arm was back."

"No." Harley shook her head. "It had to be some kind of illusion."

"Maybe," admitted Billie. "But if it was, it sure was a painful one." She opened her eyes and went on with her story. "On other days they found different ways to hurt me. They put a bag over my head and suffocated me. They had this torch thing they used to burn me. Sometimes they shocked me with electricity." Her voice grew softer. "Sometimes they did all of it together. But no matter how badly they hurt me, I would be all right the next day. No scars, or anything."

Noah felt too astonished to speak. His dreams had been terrible, but he had never dreamed anything like the horrors that Billie described. The way she spoke about them in her slow, gentle voice only seemed to make the descriptions of what had been done to her even worse. "That's awful," he blurted out. Then he winced. His words sounded so lame next to what this girl had endured.

"I don't understand," Harley said, crossing her arms over her chest. "Why would they do all this to someone? I mean, what they did to Noah had a purpose, but this doesn't make any sense."

Billie shrugged again. "I think they just wanted to see how much I could take," she explained.

"Maybe they know how human beings are put together—heart, lungs, brains, all that stuff. But they don't know how human beings really *act*. Maybe they wanted to see what I would do."

"It doesn't seem like a very good test," Harley countered. "I'd think they could come up with something better than cutting a person up—"

Noah felt a flash of irritation with Harley's interruptions. "You can't expect Billie to know what these things are up to," he broke in. "She's just another victim." He turned back to the red-haired girl. "Go on. Tell us what else you remember."

"There's not much." Billie put her elbows on her knees and cradled her heart-shaped face in her pale hands. "My whole life was just waiting to see how they were going to hurt me next. Then they took me out of my room, and one of the tall ones told me they were going to take me to another place. As soon as they put me in the van, I started thinking about Noah."

Harley stood up and brushed the dust off her jeans. "Now I *really* don't understand," she said. "How could you know anything about Noah?"

Billie's mouth dropped open in surprise. "Didn't I tell you?" She looked over at Noah. "Noah and I have met before."

Noah blinked in surprise. "We have? When?"

"In the hurting place," Billie replied. "You came

50

there. . . ." She hesitated and shook her head. "I don't know how long ago. Maybe weeks, maybe years. It was all the same there. All the same—except for you."

"You really saw me?" The idea seemed incredible to Noah. He was ready to accept that the aliens had done things to his mind, but how could he have ever seen Billie before and not remember her? "Did we talk?" he asked.

Billie nodded. "They put us in the same room once. It was so small, we had to lean against each other when we sat down. That's where you told me about Stone Harbor. You said you had been captured by the aliens many times before, but they always let you go. You said you'd help me get free." The girl frowned. "Don't you remember?"

Noah strained to recall everything he could about the dark place in his recurring, fragmented dreams. He could summon up images of the white-faced aliens, the figure of a man holding a sharp knife or scalpel, the metal table, the cold, dark room. Nowhere in those twisted memories was there anyone like Billie.

"No," he admitted at last. He felt guilty that he had made such an important promise and couldn't remember a word of it. "I'm sorry."

The disappointment on Billie's face was painfully obvious. "I guess I should have realized they'd mess with your memories. But when you were there, you seemed like you knew everything that was going on."

"I did?" Noah asked. His sense of astonishment was growing. "What did I know?"

"You told me that you were part of a breeding experiment," the red-haired girl answered. "That someone called Legion had made you—"

"Made him?" Dee interrupted, her eyes enormous behind her glasses.

Billie nodded. *"Created* you," she continued, staring intently at Noah, "to test some theories about paranormal abilities. You were supposed to be their biggest success."

Harley rolled her eyes.

Noah frowned. "Paranormal abilities? I don't have any paranormal abilities."

A buzzing sound grew in his head, like a field of crickets on a summer evening. Then came a voice. It was a bright, inhuman voice, more like a ringing bell than a person speaking. But the words were perfectly clear. *Yes,* it said, *you do.*

"What was that?" Noah gasped.

"What?" Harley asked.

"That voice. That sound."

Harley shook her head. "I didn't hear anything."

There was a movement in the shadows that made Noah tense, but then he realized that it was only Dee, shifting nervously.

"You hearing voices, Templer?" Dee asked. "Maybe it's time you got some rest."

Billie sat up straighter in her chair and pushed the blanket away from her shoulders. "It was me," she said. "Here, I'll do it again."

The buzzing sound rose around Noah. *You taught me,* said the bell-like voice. *You taught me how we could speak with only our minds.*

Noah laughed aloud. "That's amazing!" he cried.

Harley walked toward him. "I don't understand," she said. "What's going on?"

"It's Billie. She can communicate without talking." He looked at Billie. "Show them what you can do."

The girl shook her head. "I can't," she said. "You were the one who taught me to do it. I can talk only to you."

"I really taught you that?" Noah shook his head in wonder. He got up and moved closer to Billie. "You think I can learn to do it again?"

Billie nodded and smiled. She took both of his hands in hers. "You taught me. Now I guess it's my turn to teach you."

Dee covered her eyes with her hands. "This is a little too wacky for me," she whined.

"What about your escape?" Harley asked Billie sharply.

The red-haired girl looked up at Harley. "What?"

53

"You still haven't told us how you got away from Legion." Harley leaned against a wall and crossed her arms over her chest again. "Or how you ended up here."

Billie released her hold on Noah's hands. "It's all part of the same thing, really," she said in her soft southern drawl. "They decided to move me. I don't know why, or where they were going . . . they never bothered to tell me." She passed a hand over her eyes. "I couldn't see anyone or anything, but they made me walk a long way. Then I heard a motor start, and I realized that I was inside a vehicle."

The images were so clear in Noah's mind, he wondered if there was more to Billie's paranormal abilities than just sending words. It was almost as if there were a movie playing in his skull, bringing him terrible pictures to go with the girl's quiet narration. He could almost feel the dark blindfold wrapped around his own face and hear the rumble of a motor.

"We drove for . . ." Billie's voice trailed away. "I don't know how long we drove. A long time. Then I suddenly got the feeling that Noah was close."

"How did you know?" asked Harley.

"I just knew," Billie said firmly. "The next time I felt the van stop, I kicked and pushed and managed to get the door off."

Dee piped up, asking, "You're sure it was a van?"

"I saw it after I got the blindfold off," Billie replied with a nod. "Then I ran into the woods, and then Noah found me, and, well . . ." She shrugged her bare shoulders. "Here I am."

"Yes, here you are," Harley repeated. There was a flat quality to her voice that Noah had never heard before. "Do you have any idea how long you were a prisoner? Do you remember the date when they first took you?"

Billie stared off into the shadows, her face a mask of concentration. "I was fourteen," she said finally. "I remember that much." She hesitated, then named a date. "Does that sound right?"

"Two years ago," said Noah. There was a sick feeling in the pit of his stomach. His short visits to that dark place had given him nightmares that had wrecked his life. This girl had endured two years of torture at the hands of those creatures.

"I guess you're sixteen now," said Dee. "We'll have to throw a party sometime."

Billie gave a little laugh, but the expression on her face was anything but happy. The laugh quickly died, and she suddenly slumped down in her chair.

Noah jumped to his feet and leaned over her chair. "Are you all right?"

"I'm fine," Billie said weakly. "I'm just so awfully tired."

Dee stood up. "We should let her rest," she said. "We can find out more tomorrow."

Reluctantly Noah nodded. "I guess so. Maybe I should stay here tonight, just in case."

"I don't think you need to do that," said Harley. "I'll be here in case something goes wrong."

Noah looked down at Billie. "Is there anything I can get for you?"

The girl shook her head. "No. I just need to get some sleep. I'll be fine." A smile came to her tired face. "Now that I've found you."

From across the room, Dee made a choking sound.

"What's wrong with you?" asked Noah.

"Nothing," said Dee. "Something just went down the wrong tube."

"Okay." Noah stood up. "I guess we'd better get going." He took one last look at Billie and then turned to face Harley. "I put a few groceries in the fridge this weekend, and all the appliances seem to be running okay. There's a little store about five miles down the road. If you feel like getting adventurous, there's a little jon boat down by the docks. The keys are in the kitchen." He paused, then shrugged. "That's it, I guess. If you need anything else, you can call me from the pay phone at the store."

Harley nodded. "I think we'll manage."

Billie stirred in her chair. "Are you hiding somewhere close by?" she asked.

"I'm not really hiding," said Noah. "I'm staying at home."

"At home?" Billie sat bolt upright. "With your parents?"

Noah nodded. "Yeah. Sure."

There was a look of awful distress on Billie's heart-shaped face. "But Noah, don't you remember what you told me about them?"

"I don't remember telling you anything," Noah reminded her. "What did I say about my parents?"

Billie drew in a sharp breath. "You told me they were working for Legion," she replied.

FIVE

Harley lay in the bed and stared into the darkness.

It was terribly quiet in the cabin, quiet enough that Harley could hear the soft sound of Billie's breathing from where she was sleeping downstairs. The darkness was as complete as the quiet. Not the least hint of light entered the tiny loft bedroom where Harley was trying to get some rest. Noah had brought a fresh set of sheets and blankets, but the room still bore the odor of mothballs and mold. Harley was beginning to feel as though she had been buried alive.

When she was unable to bear the oppressive atmosphere a moment longer, Harley threw off her sheets. Working quietly in the darkness, she gathered her few things and stuffed them into a battered backpack. She picked up the revolver her father had left behind. Even in the darkness, the gun had a certain weight to it—a certain feel of danger. She wrapped it carefully inside a shirt, tied in a sock the six bullets she had, and shoved it all inside the backpack. Lastly she added her father's journal to the pack, promising herself that she would find time to read its confusing contents very soon. Then she slung the pack over her

59

shoulder and made her way down the ladder from the loft.

Embers lingered in the downstairs fireplace. Their red light poured through the dark room like spilled blood. Harley walked softly across the room and stood for a moment near Billie.

The red-haired girl had said she was too tired to climb the ladder up to the loft bedroom, so she had curled up on the couch. Asleep, Billie looked even younger than her sixteen years. She lay on her side, with her knees drawn up almost to her chin. Her pale arms dangled from the side of the couch, fingers dancing in some nightmare task. She made soft noises in her sleep, like the cries of a tiny, injured animal.

Harley wanted to hate the girl, but she couldn't quite manage it. Noah was so excited to have found her. Harley felt jealous and probably would feel that way for a long time, but she was glad to see Noah excited about something. And if Billie had gone through one-tenth of the misery she claimed to have experienced, she deserved a little sympathy. Harley reached down and gently adjusted Billie's blanket, then left her sleeping.

Harley found a notepad on the kitchen counter. She took a piece of paper from the top of the pad and started to leave a message. She had worked out a story about going to visit her aunt. It wasn't a

particularly good story—Noah would probably be
suspicious. Harley got as far as "Dear Noah" and
then stopped. Even on paper, she was no good at
lying.

She crumpled the sheet of paper and tossed it
into the trash. She would go without a note. If
everything went well, she would be gone for only
a couple of days. Noah would probably be too
busy thinking about Billie to worry about anything else.

If everything *didn't* go well, then what Noah
thought was going to be the least of Harley's
problems.

Dawn was beginning to turn the eastern sky
gray when Harley eased the cabin door open
and slipped outside. With the faint glow to
light her way, she followed the path through
the maze of stones up to the highway, where
she had left her bike. The motorcycle started
easily, and Harley headed out, her headlight
cutting the morning gloom as she drove away
from Noah and Stone Harbor—the last place
she had seen her father.

The trip to New York was long, but the hours
passed without any real incident. Most of the roads
were stretches of dull, straight interstate highway.
Harley stopped only for gas and to eat at a couple
of roadside diners. Even though she had two thousand dollars in her backpack, she was careful to

spend as little as possible. When it came time to use the money, she was afraid she might need every penny.

She was also careful to keep her speed down to whatever the local signs demanded. Even so, she kept a nervous eye on her rearview mirror. Cain's fake identification cards might be good, but she was in no particular hurry to test them out.

With two hours left in her journey, traffic began to thicken. An hour later the road was packed like rush hour anywhere else. A fitful storm came up, driving equal measures of rain and slushy snow against the plastic face shield on Harley's helmet. She shivered and made a mental note to buy a better jacket as soon as she could. Her old leather riding jacket had been lost along with the rest of her things. Dee's loaner was just not up to keeping Harley warm while riding a motorcycle in cold rain.

When the dark outline of New York became visible through the thin rain, Harley felt a deep unease. The city was big. She had known it would be, of course, but it was big in a way she hadn't expected. Harley had been through Los Angeles several times, but L.A. was spread out in miles of strip malls, fast-food places, and auto dealerships. It was like a lot of suburbs all pressed together.

New York looked nothing like that. It was massive. So many tall, hulking buildings were pressed into such a tight space that Harley couldn't believe the ground could support them. All the steel and concrete seemed poised right on the lip of the harbor, and she half expected the earth to sag, sinking the whole place. Looking down the shadowed canyons between those giant buildings across the river made her feel very small and very alone.

Before she reached the George Washington Bridge, Harley pulled off the highway and fished out the packet of material that Cain had provided. There were maps of the city on several scales, all indicating the position of the building Harley was to visit. She traced her fingers along the map and found the nearest street linking her to the building from the West Side Highway. West Street. With butterflies in her stomach, she pulled onto the road and headed toward her final destination.

It took over an hour to reach the place Cain had indicated. The neighborhood was not a area of gleaming skyscrapers or even a good office district. Most of the buildings were low, aging warehouses, some with boarded-up windows, others with paint peeling from their sides.

Harley had to check the map twice more before she found the building she was looking for; then, once she found it, she checked the notes again. The address was correct. Even so, she barely could believe this was the building that had so interested Cain. The agent might be very clever at some things, but this time he had to have made a mistake.

It was an old brick building, four stories tall, wedged into a block of lower, even older, warehouses. There were black smudges around the windows of the building that made it look as if there had once been a fire inside. Timeworn advertisements clung to the smoke-stained brick walls. Harley could make out the worn shape of a beer can on one shabby poster, but the painted label had faded so completely she couldn't make out what brand had once thought this was a good place to leave an ad.

Across the street from the building was a small playground. The equipment in the playground was rusty, and it was overgrown with weeds. Not a single child played on the limp swings or dared the sagging jungle gym—most likely no one played there even in good weather. The place wasn't pretty, but it did provide a good spot for Harley to sit and watch the building.

She steered her motorcycle onto the cracked sidewalk and killed the engine. She pushed through knee-high weeds to a deserted sliding board and chained up her bike. Then she took another look at the pages Cain had given her.

The maps were good, and all the directions for finding the building were very clear. But now that she had found the place, her next step was terribly vague. According to the instructions, she was to "observe and take appropriate action." As far as Harley was concerned, the only appropriate action was getting on her bike and heading directly back to Stone Harbor. But she had made a deal with Cain. Harley took a seat on the edge of a warped merry-go-round and began her observation of the building that was supposed to be controlled by Unit 17.

There wasn't much to observe. The curtainless windows of the old building glared down at Harley like banks of blind eyes. Bouts of rain passed in brief, fitful storms, lasting just long enough to leave Harley damp and chilled. At the building next door, trucks came and went, delivering sides of beef that were hauled inside by a row of men in bloodstained coveralls. It was easy to see why no children wanted to play in the playground—the whole neighborhood smelled like a slaughterhouse.

Harley had waited over thirty minutes before a group of people emerged from the Unit 17 building. The only thing worth noting about the group was that they were dressed a little better than other people Harley had seen in the neighborhood.

There were two men and two women, none of them looked like really anything special. Harley watched the group walk down the block and climb into a gray sedan. In a few seconds they had driven away down the rain-slick street. Harley made a note of the time and jotted down a basic description of the people.

After another twenty minutes had gone by without any activity, Harley began to get bored. She fished in her pack and pulled out her father's journal. The tiny volume didn't look like much. The cover was made from leather so worn it had become fuzzy. Anybody could buy one like it at a discount store for no more than a couple of bucks. But inside, the small pages were crammed with tiny, cramped writing that recorded ten years of her father's life.

Most of the contents were a mystery to Harley. She had glanced at only a few of the pages before Cain had taken the book. Even those few pages had been able to show that there was a connection between her father's work and Noah's dreams. Now that she had the book in her hands again, Harley intended to learn everything she could. She opened the journal to the first page and began to read.

July 24—P's natural ability gtr than expected. Everyone vry excited. Trans-alpha patterns off chart. Paratheta also vry high. A reexamination of goals is called for, but M insists we press ahead.

July 25—P agreed to accept enhancement. I still have reservations. Urged her to reconsider. M vry angry. He agreed to complete remote observation series before enhancement put in place. Results continue to be encouraging.

Harley stopped for a moment and flipped through the pages. The first two entries seemed typical. Harley frowned as she tried to puzzle out the meaning of the little pieces of text. Her father had always told her that he worked on radar systems. But whatever was recorded in this book, she didn't think it had anything to do with radar.

A movement across the street caught her eye. Another group of men and women had emerged from the building. Harley examined them for a moment and made a quick note of the time. She was about to go back to reading when something grabbed her attention.

The people leaving the building had nothing really distinctive about them. In fact, they were almost aggressively plain. They all had hair of a sort of mousy brown shade. None was particularly tall or especially short. They wore dark clothing that looked fine but not too fancy. At first glance, they seemed like the kind of people you passed in the street in every big city.

The only trouble was, Harley was fairly convinced that they were the same four people who had come out of the building thirty minutes earlier. She watched as this new group moved down the street and climbed into a car—a blue van this time—and rolled away.

They *are* the same people, Harley decided. Somehow they must have come back to the building and entered through a door Harley couldn't see—only to exit again and leave in the blue van. Maybe their first car had broken down.

Whatever the explanation, Harley watched the building with renewed interest. Twenty minutes later a third group appeared. Two men. Two women. Everything just the same as before. They walked down to the corner and hopped into a white car.

"What's going on here?" Harley whispered under her breath. She waited until this third group had driven out of sight, then she walked up to the sidewalk across from the building.

It was still simply an ugly old building, but Harley no longer thought that Cain was wrong about this place. No matter how drab the building looked on the outside, something strange was definitely going on behind all that dirty brick.

Now all she had to do was figure out how to get inside.

The answer arrived ten minutes later. A man on a bicycle pulled up, hopped off his bike, and ran inside with a small package in one hand. A few seconds later he came out, got back on his bike, and pedaled away.

Harley crouched down behind the merry-go-round, opened her backpack, and carefully unwrapped her father's gun. She found the sockful of bullets and poured the coppery cylinders into her palm. They slotted snugly into the chambers. Once the gun was fully loaded, Harley jammed it down into the back of her jeans and pulled her shirt and jacket over it. She took a few experimental steps. It felt odd to have the cold metal pressing into the small of her back, but at least the gun seemed secure.

Her weapon prepared, Harley headed over to a Dumpster at the side of the road. She grimaced at the smell that rose from the trash heaped inside, but she searched through the mess until she found a large manila envelope. There were some pretty disgusting dark stains on the paper. Harley wrinkled her nose and did her best to ignore them. She tucked the envelope under her arm and marched into the building.

The foyer of the building was just as disappointing as the outside. The Unit 17 base at Tulley Hill had been filled with all sorts of exotic materials and high-tech gadgets. This place had nothing more high-tech than a light bulb. An older, official-looking woman sat behind a small, battered metal desk that was topped by a single green-shaded lamp. On the wall was a black plastic chart with the names of people who were supposed to be working in the building.

Harley took a quick glance at the chart and walked up to the desk. She tried to look bored, as if this were something she did every day. "Delivery for Clint Thompson," she told the woman behind the desk.

The woman looked at Harley over the top of a pair of wire-rimmed glasses. "You want to leave it here?" she asked.

Harley shook her head. "I'm supposed to take it up."

The woman shrugged. "Whatever. He's on the fourth floor." She picked up a clipboard and shoved it across the desk. "Sign in."

Harley made an illegible scrawl on the clipboard and moved over to the elevators. Her nerves were humming like guitar strings. It was too easy.

The elevator opened, and Harley climbed inside. Even when the doors closed, she still felt exposed. There could be hidden cameras anywhere.

The elevator was as old as the rest of the building, and it moved upward with a slow groan. Every time it jerked or bumped, Harley was afraid it would stop. She could be trapped in this tiny metal chamber, at the mercy of Unit 17.

Finally the light for the fourth floor lit up and the doors slid open—to reveal another disappointment. Two rows of desks stretched out on either side of a narrow aisle. A dozen men and women sat at the desks with phones pressed to their ears.

A man near the front put his hand over the mouthpiece. "Yeah?" he called. "Can I help you?"

"Sorry," Harley replied. "Wrong floor."

She stepped back into the elevator and pressed the button for the third floor. It didn't light. She scowled at the button and pressed again, with no effect. The light for the second floor wouldn't work, either. Only when Harley pressed the button for the first floor did a bell sound and the doors squeak shut.

The elevator had been happy to take Harley to the fourth floor, but it didn't seem interested in going anywhere else. As it began to move downward she wondered about the woman in the lobby. What if the receptionist was trained to always send people to the fourth floor? The middle floors of the building could hold anything, anything at all, and no one would ever know.

Frustrated, Harley punched the button for the third floor again and again, but the elevator kept going right on past. She moved her finger to the second-floor button. Unit 17 was here. She knew they were here. The elevator gave a shudder and stopped at floor two.

Harley braced herself as the doors slid open. If she could get a good look at what was inside . . .

But she didn't get the chance. As soon as the doors opened, people poured into the elevator. All Harley saw of the second floor was a flat wall covered in clean white paint.

Five people got into the elevator with Harley. The first four were all too familiar: two men, two women. Brown hair. Dark suits. They could have been the same people she had already seen leave the building three times.

Harley supposed it was possible that they were coming back into the building by some other route. But she didn't believe that. These people might look just like the ones she had seen before, but they were different.

An image of Coach Rocklin came into Harley's mind. Coach Rocklin had been the track coach back in Stone Harbor, but she had turned out to be a Unit 17 agent planted to watch over Harley. When Harley had injured her in a life-or-death struggle, Coach Rocklin had bled something that was definitely not blood. Not *human* blood, anyway.

Harley pressed herself against the back of the elevator. The revolver jammed into her skin as she flattened herself against the wall. Harley slipped one hand behind herself to place it closer to the gun. These people could be like Coach Rocklin, filled with metal and clear fluids instead of bones and blood. Even thinking about it made Harley's stomach tighten in disgust. She didn't want these things to touch her.

The last man to get into the elevator was unlike the first four. Harley didn't get a look at his face as he entered the car. She saw only that he was a stocky man wearing an ugly lemon yellow suit. Definitely not one of the clone brigade.

"We expect to have four new customers by the end of the week," said one of the women.

"That's the target," replied one of the duplicate men.

There was a tone in their voices that made Harley push herself further against the elevator wall. The sound was oily. Mechanical. It reinforced Harley's feeling that these were *things,* not people.

"We had better exceed those targets," said the man in the yellow suit. His voice was hard and demanding but human. He turned his head slightly. For a moment Harley saw a large, off-center nose and a thin mustache above even thinner lips.

A shock of recognition went through her. *Braddock.*

Harley shifted to put one of the duplicates between herself and the stocky man. Her pulse pounded so loudly in her ears that it drowned out the conversation of the people in the elevator.

Braddock had been the commander of the Tulley Hill facility. He was the one who had first told Harley that her father was going away on an assignment, and who had captured Harley when she had tried to search the base. She had thought the Unit 17 commander had been killed in the series of explosions and gunfire that had nearly destroyed Tulley Hill. But here he was, obviously alive and standing not five feet away.

Now Harley wished she had followed Cain's advice and done something to disguise herself. She and the base commander had been almost nose to nose more than once. If he got a good look at Harley, Braddock was certain to remember her. She prayed that Braddock wouldn't get a good look.

The bell sounded, and the doors opened on the first floor. Harley pressed herself back into the corner as the other five people filed out. Harley sighed in relief as Braddock disappeared from view. She waited until the doors had begun to close again before she dared step out into the lobby.

Braddock was out of sight.

Harley walked to the center of the lobby and looked toward the entrance. She was just in time to see the last of the duplicates slipping out the door.

"Did you find Mr. Thompson?" asked the woman behind the desk.

Harley jumped at the voice and had to swallow hard before she could reply. "Yeah. No problem."

The woman gave Harley a hard look. "Why don't you wait here a moment?" she said. "I believe we might have something that needs to be delivered."

"No, I've got to run." Harley hurried to the door.

"You need to sign out!" called the woman behind the desk.

Harley ignored her. She emerged onto the street just in time to see Braddock's yellow suit climbing into a red station wagon half a block away.

Her instructions had been to observe and take appropriate action. Up until this moment, Harley hadn't known quite what that meant, but now she knew exactly what she should do.

She sprinted across the street and unchained her motorcycle. By the time the station wagon had worked its way out of its tight parking place, Harley had the Sportster started and her helmet on her head. She pulled the gun from the back of her jeans and jammed it into her backpack, but this time she kept it loaded and ready.

Braddock was the one person she knew was involved in her father's disappearance—and he was not going to get away.

By dinnertime, Noah felt certain that what Billie had said must be true: His parents were part of the conspiracy.

He sat in the woods across the street from his house and watched as his parents got ready to go out for the evening. Noah could see their shadows moving across the windows as they walked back and forth through the big house. A day ago he would have been happy to see them. Now he felt as if he was going to be sick.

It was so obvious. He couldn't imagine why he hadn't seen it before. Twenty years ago Noah's father had been a poor fisherman. Then, about the time Noah was born, he had sold his boat and made a series of brilliant investments. Overnight the Templers had gone from having trouble putting bread on the table to being one of the wealthiest families in Stone Harbor.

At least, that was what Noah had been told—and had always believed.

But he had never seen his father do much more than manage his money. There was no sign of any great investment expertise. His father spent more time watching baseball than he did looking at stock reports. How would a fisherman know enough to become an overnight millionaire? How could an old fishing boat provide enough money to do anything? Noah didn't believe it could.

But Legion obviously had money. If Noah really was the product of a Legion breeding experiment, as Billie had suggested, then maybe his parents had been working for Legion all along. Maybe they weren't even his parents. Noah recalled the words that Josh McQuinn—or the Legion creature Noah had always believed to be Josh—had said before he died: "I placed you with your family." Noah suddenly felt cold all over. The lies were layered so deeply that he could no longer tell what was real.

The garage door suddenly begin to rise. His father's Lexus backed out of the driveway, turned, and drove down the street.

Noah watched the car's taillights disappear over a hill. He thought for a moment about following. His parents had said they were going out for dinner, but there was no way of knowing where they were really going. He decided he could wait. His parents didn't know that Noah was on to them. He could wait.

Tonight he needed to talk to Billie. He got into his car and drove thirty miles per hour over the speed limit all the way from his house to the cabin. Even so, it was completely dark by the time he arrived.

The days were getting awfully short. He skidded to a halt at the side of the road and pulled another box of groceries out of the trunk. Since there were two people staying at the cabin instead of only one, he'd thought it would be a good idea to bring a little extra food.

The lights from the cabin cast a warm yellow glow through the dark trees. Noah picked his way down the narrow path. Holding the groceries in both hands, he kicked on the door. "Are you guys in there?" he called.

There was the sound of soft steps, and then Billie opened the door. She looked up at him and smiled. "I'm so glad to see you," she said.

Noah almost dropped the groceries. The worn, dirt-smeared girl he had literally picked up off the ground the day before had been completely transformed. Her hair glowed like strands of copper. Her skin was scrubbed clean and was smooth as ivory. She wore only a large sweatshirt, which covered her from her neck to just above her knees, but the opening at the top of the garment was wide enough to slip down and reveal the curve of her white shoulder. Her face wasn't just delicate, it was beautiful.

Billie frowned. "Are you all right?"

"Um . . . yeah," said Noah. He realized that he was staring. "You mind if I come in?"

"Of course not," said Billie. "After all, it's your

house." She stepped aside. Noah stumbled on the doorsill, but he managed to get inside without dropping the groceries.

The interior of the cabin surprised him almost as much as Billie had. The cabin had always been sturdy, but it had also been dusty, disused, and a little gloomy. Now it was so clean that it shone. The air was full of the scents of wood polish and glass cleaner. Every light in the cabin glowed brightly, including a few Noah didn't remember being there. The normally dim little room had become a cheerful, welcoming home.

"Wow," said Noah. He put the groceries down on the counter and turned around slowly, awed by the gleaming wood. "You guys must have worked all day on this place."

Billie shrugged. Her sweatshirt shifted to the side and threatened to slide completely off her shoulder. She grabbed it with one hand and pulled it back up. "This is a nice place. All it needed was a little cleaning."

"But where'd you get the stuff to do all this?" asked Noah. "All I brought was orange juice, bread, and some cheese. I don't think you cleaned the windows with cheddar."

"No." Billie grinned. "I just walked down to that little store and bought a few things."

"Walked?" Noah looked back at Billie, noticing how her smooth legs stuck out from the bottom of the sweatshirt. "It's got to be five miles up there. Why didn't Harley drive her bike?"

Billie's red lips formed into a little O of surprise. She raised a hand to her mouth. "You don't know."

"Know what?"

"Harley's not here," Billie said through her fingers. "She's been gone all day."

Fear knifed through Noah like a blade of ice. "Someone took her," he said. "We've got to go find her!" He started for the door, but Billie hurried to get in front of him.

"It wasn't like that," she said. "Nobody came in here and took her. She left on her own."

Noah cocked his head. "Why should Harley leave?"

Billie looked down at the floor. "I think it might be my fault."

"Your fault?" Noah frowned. "Did you do something?"

"No, but . . ." Billie nodded without looking up. "Last night, after you left, Harley seemed really upset. Then this morning she got up and left before we really had a chance to talk. I think . . . I think she was upset that you brought me here."

Noah tried to remember what Harley had said the previous night. She had questioned Billie's story pretty intensely, hard enough that Noah had gotten angry about it. But Harley hadn't said anything about leaving. She couldn't be *that* jealous of Billie. After all, there was nothing romantic going on between Harley and Noah. Not really.

"I can't believe she'd actually go," he said. Noah fell into a chair and put his head in his hands. "Where could she be? Her father was the only family she had, and he's missing."

Billie knelt down beside Noah's chair. "Are you sure?" she said.

"Sure about what?"

"About Harley not having anyone else. Maybe she had other family somewhere you didn't know about. Or maybe some friends she could stay with."

Noah thought for a second. "She never told me about anyone else."

"Did she tell you everything?"

"I thought so," said Noah. He ran his hands through his blond hair. "Now I'm not so sure."

Billie put her hands on his arm. "Maybe she'll come back," she said. "Maybe she just went to see one of the others in your group."

"In our group?" Noah looked up, puzzled. "What others? There's me and Harley, and I guess you could count Dee."

"Don't forget the ones you were telling me about yesterday," Billie reminded him. "The ones you talked to on the Internet."

"Oh, those guys." Noah shook his head. "Harley doesn't even know them. She thinks I'm nuts for telling them as much as I do."

"But *you* know them," said Billie. "At least, you know how to get in touch with them. Right?"

"Yeah," said Noah. "Why? Do you think they could help us find Harley?"

"Maybe." Billie shrugged, and once again she had to act quickly to keep the loose sweatshirt from sliding off her shoulder. "But maybe we shouldn't try to find her. Harley might just have wanted to get away from all this for a while. Maybe she went somewhere to relax."

Noah wished he could believe Billie was right, but he was still shocked at the very idea of Harley leaving. He had no idea what else she might do. Could Harley really be upset over Noah's bringing Billie to the cabin? He couldn't imagine that she would have wanted him to leave Billie without helping her.

Billie moved around to the front of Noah's chair and took both his hands with hers. "What if we get out of here for a little while?" she suggested. "You could take me into Stone Harbor. I'd like to see a little more of the town."

"Sure." Noah nodded. "I guess we could do that."

"Great," said Billie. "Wait here a second. I'll get dressed." She gave his hands a squeeze, hopped up, and hurried across the cabin on bare feet.

Noah felt the beginnings of a headache thrumming at his temples. Harley's arrival in Stone Harbor had been the trigger that had revealed the edges of Unit 17, Legion, and the vast secrets hidden behind the facade of everyday life. Now Billie had come, and the world was unraveling again. Between Harley's disappearance and what he had found out about his parents, Noah wasn't sure what to think about anything.

Noah had been with Harley for only a few weeks, but he had come to depend on her. She was smart, probably smarter than he was. She was also a little more careful than Noah—a trait that had probably kept them both alive. The only thing that really got Harley upset was her concern for her missing father.

"Maybe that's it," Noah said aloud.

"What?" Billie called from somewhere behind him.

"Maybe Harley went to look for her father." Noah turned around in his chair. "Did she say anything last night? Maybe something you said made her think of a place where she could look for her dad."

"No. I don't think so." Billie walked over. She was wearing a dark green sweater and a short skirt. Like the sweatshirt she had worn before, the clothes were several sizes too large for Billie's slim figure, but there was something striking about the folds of green cloth set against her pale skin and copper-bright hair.

"Where did you get those clothes?" Noah asked.

"Do you like them?" Billie picked at the sweater. "They were up in the loft, where Harley slept last night. I hope she won't mind if I borrow them."

Noah shrugged. "They probably came from Dee, anyway. Most of Harley's stuff was lost."

"What *happened* to Harley, anyway?" Billie asked. "How did she lose her dad and all her things? Did Legion hold her prisoner, they way it did you and me?"

"No," said Noah. "Not exactly." He got up from his chair. "Come on. We can talk about it on the way to town."

Billie took his hand as they walked up the dark path to the car. Her fingers were small and cool, and they somehow felt completely natural in Noah's grip. Noah felt a tingle of excitement at her touch. The feeling was so intense that he almost drew away. No girl had made him this nervous since he was twelve years old.

Once in the car, Noah turned around and drove toward the coast. "Are you hungry?" he asked.

Billie nodded. "I haven't taken time to do much cooking today. I kept thinking that Harley might come back, and I didn't know whether to cook for one person or two."

"Good," said Noah. "I mean, it's good that you're hungry, not that Harley's gone. There's a restaurant I know between here and Stone Harbor. It doesn't look like much, but if you like seafood, you're going to like this place."

"I love seafood," Billie replied. "It sounds wonderful."

They reached the highway and headed up the coast. A full moon was peeking out between fast-moving clouds. Its pale light seemed bright enough that Noah could have turned off the headlights. With the moon sailing overhead, and occasional glimpses of the dark sea off to the right, it was a beautiful night for a drive.

They were a mile south of the restaurant when Billie suddenly grabbed Noah's arm. "Who's that?" she said, pointing to a figure moving along the side of the road.

Noah turned his head just in time to see the person as they went past. He couldn't make out much, but he saw the gleam of a yellow rain slicker and rubberized hat. "From the clothes, it's probably just some old fisherman. There are a lot of them around here who still dress like that."

Billie twisted around in her seat, staring back at the walking man. "There's something wrong with him."

"What do you mean?"

The red-haired girl shook her head. "I don't know. I didn't get a good look. But I get a bad feeling from him."

Noah glanced into his mirror. He could just make out the figure behind them. "Do you think we should do something?"

"No," Billie said softly. She turned around. "No, I guess not."

The Fiddler's Crab was a odd mix of food and music. Depending on the day and the time, the music could be anything from bluegrass cranked out of an old jukebox to classical played live by a string quartet. The food was always the same—good. In the summer, the Crab was a big favorite with tourists. In the winter, when the population of Stone Harbor dipped down to almost nothing, the locals felt it was safe to return.

Noah had been telling the truth when he said it wasn't fancy. There were candles on the tables, but the tablecloths were as mismatched as the music, and the waitresses dressed in jeans.

"You ever have soft-shell crabs?" he asked when they were seated near the front of the restaurant.

Billie looked thoughtful for a moment. "If I have, I don't remember." She gave a nervous laugh. "I guess there are some good things about losing most of your memory. You get to have a whole new set of first times."

"Did you think of anything new today?" Noah asked. "Did you remember anything more about your family?"

"I'm not sure," Billie replied. "Something about a Fort Mac-something." She frowned and shrugged. "Does that make any sense?"

"Maybe your dad worked at a military base, like Harley's," Noah suggested.

"I'm not sure." Billie stared down at her clasped hands on the table, and Noah suddenly felt a powerful wave of sadness radiating from the petite girl.

Noah reached across the table and put his hand over hers for a moment. "Don't worry," he said. "Your memory will come back soon. You just wait and see."

She raised her head and smiled at him. "I hope so," she whispered.

The waitress came and collected their orders. After she left, Billie looked across the table, the candlelight gleaming in her turquoise eyes. "You were going to tell me about Harley."

"Right," said Noah. He glanced around to make sure no one was sitting too close. The restaurant was all but empty. Noah leaned forward and spoke in a soft voice. "Have you ever heard of Unit Seventeen?"

Billie shook her head. "What's that?"

"It's a secret military organization," Noah explained. "I think they started as one of those projects the government is always hiding from everybody. Only this time the project got out of hand. Now Unit Seventeen runs itself. Kind of like Legion."

"Another one?" said Billie. "Like having Legion wasn't bad enough!"

"Right. Well, Unit Seventeen used to run a base outside of Stone Harbor. Harley's dad worked there."

"You mean he was part of them?" Billie asked.

Noah began to shake his head, then stopped. "Maybe. He worked for them, but Harley said he didn't know what they were really about. A couple of weeks ago he disappeared. The base told Harley that her dad was away on assignment. She didn't believe it. Then she talked to me, and together we did a little poking around on the base."

Billie's eyes widened. "You and Harley broke into a secret base? I'm surprised they didn't kill you."

Noah nodded. "Me too. They caught us, and I think they would have killed us, but that's when Legion broke in and started tearing up the base." He leaned back in his seat. "We escaped. And now the base is gone."

"Wow," Billie said softly. "You two have really been through something. I can see why you're worried about her taking off."

"That's not even half of it," said Noah. "When

we get back to the cabin, I'll have to tell you what else went on."

Billie nodded. "Good. I want to know everything I can. I'll need to if I'm going to help."

Noah looked away. For just a moment he felt a nagging surge of suspicion. He and Harley had guarded their secrets, and now Noah was giving them away too fast.

"What's wrong?" asked Billie.

"Nothing," Noah said quickly. "It's just that I—" He glanced over at Billie, and as soon as their eyes met he realized it was going to be all right. He wasn't telling everyone. He was only telling Billie, and he simply felt—with more certainty than he'd ever felt before in his life—that she could be trusted. Harley wouldn't mind. "Nothing's wrong," Noah said with a smile.

The waitress arrived with steaming plates of crabs, baked potatoes, and warm rolls. The crabs were still sizzling, and their arrival was accompanied by the wonderful smell of spices and drawn butter. For the next few minutes they concentrated on the food.

After her first bite of crab, Billie looked up and smiled. "You were right," she said. "It's delici . . ." Her voice trailed away. She sat frozen, her fork poised between her plate and her mouth.

"What is it?" asked Noah. "Is something wrong with the food?"

Billie tipped her head. "Over there," she said in a voice that was almost a moan. "They've found me."

Noah turned around in his seat and saw someone coming through the door of the Fiddler's Crab. The newcomer was tall, dressed in a yellow rain slicker and a matching cap. Under the brim of the cap, there was nothing visible but two glowing red sparks set into a space of incredible, impenetrable darkness.

"Run!" shouted Billie. "We have to get away!" She stood up and grabbed Noah by the sleeve. "Come on!"

The thing in the raincoat swung slowly from left to right. When its glowing eyes turned toward Noah and Billie, they froze in a vermilion stare. A deep groan issued from the creature. It lumbered toward them across the floor, pushing tables and chairs aside.

Noah scrambled to his feet. "What is it?"

"A dark one," Billie said quickly. "Hurry. We've got to get away."

A waitress appeared from the kitchen. "What's going—" That was all she managed to get out before the dark one whirled and struck her with a backhanded blow. The woman was lifted off her feet and flung twenty feet across the room. She crashed to the floor among broken chairs and shattered plates.

Noah seized a knife from the table. "Go on," he called to Billie. "Get out of here!" He jumped forward, waving the knife through the air in front of the dark creature.

The red eyes shone down on Noah. Though Noah was well over six feet tall, this thing loomed several inches taller. Nothing but darkness showed through the seams of its coat, but it seemed to have the bulk of a football lineman.

The creature swung a black paw toward Noah. The blow whistled through the air in front of Noah's chin. With it came a wind that was as cold and biting as any gale from the Arctic.

Noah backed away, wielding the knife. The dark thing took a step forward. It shoved past the table where Noah and Billie had been sitting. Plates shattered on the floor, and crabs fell against the tiles with soft plops. The shadow man kept right on coming.

"Be careful!" Billie called from behind Noah. "Don't let it touch you."

"I'm trying!" Noah held up the knife again. It was not a particularly large knife, really more suited to slicing a potato than fighting, but it was the only weapon Noah had. "Stay back," he said to the dark shape. "I'll use this if I have to."

The creature didn't seem impressed. It reached for Noah, stretching out fingers made of pure shadow.

Noah swung the knife. The blade cut through the front of the raincoat. It was a shallow slice, but it tore the yellow material of the coat wide open. Immediately the temperature in the restaurant dropped by ten degrees. Fog formed around the shadow man as the coat opened to reveal more darkness within.

With a sharp thrust, Noah jabbed the knife into the black form, burying the blade all the way up to the handle.

For a moment the attack seemed to have worked. The creature stopped and then stumbled backward a step. Its red eyes dimmed.

Noah glanced up at the empty face, feeling a surge of satisfaction. Then, just as quickly, he was hammered by pain. When Noah looked down at the wound he had made, he saw that frost had coated both the knife and his hand. Crystals of ice more than an inch long already grew across the back of his fingers. A thinner rime of ice was progressing up to his wrist. He stood, frozen as much by terror as by the ice, as the frost spread rapidly over his forearm and up to his elbow.

Small hands grabbed Noah by the back of his shirt. "Come on!" screamed Billie. She tugged him away from the creature just as the red glow in the thing's eyes returned to full strength. The knife, still frozen in Noah's hand, slid out of the creature's chest, trailing a stream of blue sparks behind.

Noah had a momentary inclination to stay and fight, but another glance at his frozen hand was enough to force him to his senses. He was not prepared to fight this thing. "Right," he said. "Let's get out of here."

Without a single look back, Noah followed Billie as she scrambled across the room, through the kitchen, past a startled cook, and out the back door. Then they sprinted around the building and hopped into the Mustang.

The ice began to melt and drip from Noah's right hand, but he still couldn't bend his frozen fingers or drop the frost-covered knife. He fumbled clumsily with his left hand to open the car door and climb inside. He was desperately trying to bend around the steering wheel and start the Mustang when the plate-glass window at the front of the Fiddler's Crab exploded outward.

Glass showered down on the Mustang as the dark one emerged. The coat and hat that had disguised its true nature were gone now, leaving only a form of solid black. The creature advanced across the parking lot, leaving footprints of frost in its wake.

"Go!" shouted Billie.

Noah again reached around the wheel, fumbling to insert the key with his left hand.

The creature was twenty feet away and coming closer every second. As he struggled with the key Noah noticed that even though it was standing in the bright moonlight, the dark one cast no shadow of its own. It simply *was* a shadow.

"Go!" Billie cried again. She pressed her hands against the dashboard. "Just go!"

"I'm trying!" Noah shouted back.

The key slid into the ignition, and Noah gave it an awkward twist. He pressed down the clutch and gave the gearshift a thump with his frozen right hand. Blinding pain lashed up his arm.

There was a bang from the front of the car.

Noah looked up to see that the shadow man had reached the Mustang. One dark hand was on the hood of the car. Trails of ice arced out from its finger like frozen lightning bolts.

"Please go!" screamed Billie, her voice raw with fear.

Noah slammed his foot down on the gas pedal. For a second the car didn't move. Rubber screeched as the rear wheels spun on the blacktop parking lot.

The dark one's red eyes glowed like torches.

Then the shadow man was forced aside. The Mustang shot past the creature, leaving it standing on a pad of spreading ice.

Noah's fingers thawed enough for him to push the car into second gear, then into third. Each shift cost him a bolt of pain.

A half mile down the highway, he looked back. For a moment Noah saw nothing. Then the shadow man separated from the darkness at the side of the restaurant and stepped into a pool of light from the street lamps. It crossed the parking lot to the edge of the highway and turned south. Even across the distance Noah could see the ruddy glow from the thing's eyes as it drew nearer, step by relentless step.

Noah stomped on the gas and sped away.

Harley had never been to New York before, but by ten P.M. she felt as though she knew every street.

The red station wagon had been traveling almost constantly since it had left the old building in the warehouse district over six hours ago. Harley had followed the car past the World Trade Center and the Empire State Building, all around Central Park, and past a dozen other places that she recognized from television. The sky had grown dark, the lights of the city had come on, and the station wagon had kept right on driving from one building to another.

Harley stayed a hundred yards back, careful to keep several cars between herself and the station wagon. She had been caught by red lights several times, but the traffic was dense enough that she had no trouble catching up again. If Braddock and the others inside the station wagon knew they were being followed, they had done nothing about it.

Ten times the car had stopped. Each time, one of the doors had swung open and one of the four drab duplicates got out and went into a nearby building. Then the station wagon waited, along with Harley, for ten or fifteen minutes. The man or woman who had come out climbed back into the car, and the station wagon drove on.

The car stopped at a wide variety of buildings: brownstone apartment buildings across from the park, gleaming skyscrapers, aging duplexes in Queens, and even a ratty, run-down tenement in a neighborhood so bad that Harley was afraid she would be mugged before the car started up again.

Harley had managed to snag a hot dog from a street vendor when the car was stopped outside an office building. Otherwise she hadn't been off her bike in hours.

The car was rolling down Westchester Avenue in the Bronx, moving at the same slow pace it had employed all day, when to Harley's surprise it suddenly turned onto the ramp for Interstate 95 and headed north out of the city. By the time Harley had pulled onto the interstate, the car was already up to speed and weaving through the northbound traffic. Harley twisted the throttle to keep up.

New Rochelle went past, and then they were in Connecticut. As Stanford came and went, Harley cast a worried look at her gas gauge. She hadn't put a lot of miles on the bike, but a day of waiting around with the engine idling had almost emptied her tank. If the car didn't pull over soon, her long chase was going to be for nothing.

This time fate was on Harley's side. Just past Stanford the station wagon exited the highway. Harley slid down the ramp after it. The car took two quick rights, then pulled into a small office complex, full of shiny new buildings that looked so clean Harley would have believed they were waxed daily. A neon-edged sign at the entrance to the office park read Comp-X. There was nothing to tell what Comp-X did, but it clearly looked like the kind of company that dealt in silicon and information access.

The car stopped in front of the tallest building in the group, a twenty-story tower. As far as Harley could tell, the building was closed for the day. There were only a few lights on inside, and the parking lot held only a handful of cars. Harley pulled over to the side of the road and killed her headlight. All four doors on the station wagon popped open at the same time. The four duplicates got out first, followed by Commander Braddock. Even in the dim light of the parking lot, his yellow suit was easy to spot. There was a muffled thump as all the car doors were closed in unison. Then the five people—or *almost* people—walked across the empty lot and entered the building.

Harley pulled her bike behind a screen of decorative shrubs, left her helmet behind, and crept out to where she had a good view of the building's entrance. Once again she unzipped her backpack and took out the revolver. The ugly little gun was no match for the powerful forces that Unit 17 could mount, but Harley already knew their agents weren't immune to bullets.

She peeked through the bushes. No activity could be seen though the glass doors of the lobby. Braddock and the clone brigade were gone.

Ten minutes went past. Twenty. Forty. The night began to grow colder. Harley shifted the revolver from hand to hand, blew on her bare fingers, and shuffled her feet as she tried to stay warm. Her watch didn't have a light, but she knew it had to be close to midnight.

Huge, fluffy snowflakes began to drift down from the black sky overhead. They seemed to hover for a moment in the lights at the edge of the parking lot, only to dive down and melt on the blacktop. After five more minutes, the flakes quit melting and the parking lot grew an ever-thickening blanket of snow.

Harley blinked the snow away from her eyes. She couldn't stand the cold much longer. It was time to retreat or attack. She wasn't sure how to attack, but she knew it was far too late to retreat.

"What would Noah do?" she whispered into the darkness. Noah had charged full speed ahead into the most secure areas back at Tulley Hill. If he were at this building, she thought, what would he do next?

A sarcastic answer formed in her mind: He'd take up with some little redhead and forget you were even alive. That wasn't being quite fair to Noah, but Harley was too cold to be fair. Still, she knew that Noah would never walk away from this place without taking a look inside. So she turned up the collar on her borrowed jacket, hid the revolver in the back of her jeans, and strolled through the front door of Comp-X.

She pushed through the glass doors and stepped into a cold, empty room. There wasn't even a chair to break up the open space. Harley's footsteps echoed hollowly though the room as she walked over the gleaming marble floor. At the rear of the lobby a single door broke the monotony of the white walls. The door was flat black, as dark as a rectangle of night. Mounted on the wall beside the door was a square of burnished metal. There was no keyhole, no doorknob, not even a slot for a security card.

Harley ran her hand over the door. The surface was fever-warm under her fingertips, and it felt somehow *wrong* in a way Harley couldn't quite define. She shoved against the dark panel, wondering if she might be able to push open the door. No luck. For a moment she thought of taking out the revolver and shooting the door. But even if she had been willing to make that kind of noise, with no obvious lock she didn't know where to shoot.

Instead she turned and examined the metal plate beside the dark door. It wasn't as smooth as Harley had thought. Tiny grooves cut across the face of the metal in an intricate looping pattern. Harley raised a hand and rubbed it across the plate, feeling the fine texture under her palm.

A light appeared above the door, and a soft chime sounded. Harley jumped back and reached for the revolver.

"Identity confirmed," said a woman's musical voice. "Davisidaro, Kathleen."

She jerked the pistol free of her jeans and pointed it toward the voice. Nothing was there but a white expanse of ceiling panels. Somewhere behind the featureless ceiling a speaker had to be hidden. Undoubtedly there was also a camera. Harley wondered if she should wave.

Hands trembling, she lowered the gun. "This is just great," she mumbled to herself. "So much for the fancy fake ID."

Harley glanced down in time to see the black door disappear. It didn't open. It didn't slide up, down, or sideways. It just disappeared like a soap bubble touched by a finger.

She swallowed hard and stared through the open space. Whatever computer system was connected to the door, it knew Harley's handprint, and it knew her name. But if it really knew who she was, why would it open the door? Harley was surely not on the list of Unit 17's favorite people.

The open door was bound to be a trap. Harley tightened her grip on the revolver. She had never shot anyone. She wasn't even sure she *could* fire the gun if it came down to putting an actual hole in an actual human being. But the snub-nosed pistol was a reassuring weight in her hand.

Gun at the ready, Harley stepped through the door. There was a soft sighing noise behind her. Harley spun around and found that the black door was back in place. She put a hand against it. Warm. Featureless. Very solid.

And from this side there was no plate to open the door.

A new smell in the air immediately told Harley that what Comp-X did wasn't strictly confined to circuit boards and transistors. There was a sharp, acrid scent in the corridor, and beneath that a mask of something musty and very unpleasant. Something that spoke of illness and medicine and bedsores. It was the smell of a hospital.

Sure enough, ten steps down the hall brought Harley to a drab green corridor lined with numbered doors. One of the doors opened, and before Harley had a chance to hide, a man appeared pushing a metal gurney. An IV stand on the corner of the cart seemed to confirm Harley's opinion of what was hidden inside the Comp-X building.

The man wore loose light blue clothing—hospital scrubs. His bald head was pale and gleaming. A tube ran from the IV and disappeared under the sleeve of his shirt. If he was surprised to see Harley, he didn't show it. He simply nodded as he passed and went on down the hallway.

After he passed, Harley realized she was still holding the revolver in her hand. She shoved it back into her jeans and followed the man around the corner. She found herself facing a broad desk, behind which sat a woman with stringy blond hair and dark circles under her eyes. Like the man who had passed Harley in the hallway, the woman behind the desk didn't seem surprised to see her. If anything, the woman looked bored.

"Name," said the woman in a flat, no-nonsense voice.

Harley hesitated. Even though the computer knew who she was, that didn't mean everyone did. She started to give the name that Cain had put on all the false identification. But the awful truth was, she couldn't remember the name Cain had given her.

"Kathleen Davisidaro," she said.

The woman nodded. She picked up a clipboard from the table and started flipping through pages. "I got a Davisidaro on five," she said. "Not Kathleen, though."

For a moment Harley was lost in confusion. Then with a shock she realized that the woman wasn't asking for her name, she was asking for the name of the patient that Harley had come to see. Not only that—there was a patient named Davisidaro on the fifth floor!

Harley had to bite her tongue to keep from shouting. It had to be her father. He was right here in this building, just a few floors away. For a fraction of a second she was so excited she wondered if she might not have some kind of heart attack. Seventeen was young for that sort of thing, but Harley's heart was beating so hard it felt as though it might break through her ribs. Right on the heels of the excitement came another emotion: *fear*. Why should her father be in a hospital? He might have been injured when the Tulley Hill facility was destroyed. Maybe he was badly hurt. Maybe he was dying.

The woman looked up from her clipboard. "Is this all you require?" she asked.

Harley cleared her throat. "Can I have the room number for the Davisidaro on the fifth floor?" she asked. She was quite proud of how calm she managed to sound.

"Certainly," said the woman. "That would be room five-nineteen." There was a quality in the blond woman's toneless voice that reminded Harley of the way the duplicate people had talked in the elevator. She wondered if there were another dozen, or another hundred, copies of this skinny, unattractive woman working at Unit 17 facilities all across the country.

Harley found an elevator at the end of the hall and pressed the button for the fifth floor. This elevator was fast and sleek, but Harley was so filled with boiling emotions that every second seemed like a year. When the door opened on the fifth floor, she came out of the elevator at a dead run. Her sprint to reach room 519 was faster than any fifty yards she had ever run on the track.

Wide wooden doors blocked the entrance to the room. Slots in the doors held a pair of buff-colored folders. Harley snatched the folders out of their slots and looked eagerly at the names written in the corners. Newcastle, T., read the cover of the first folder. On the other was the name Davisidaro, P.

Harley's heart fell so fast and hard that she thought she could feel it collide with her stomach. All her hope and fear was drowned out in a wave of disappointment.

Her father's name didn't start with *P*.

His name was Franklin. Harley didn't even *know* anyone named Davisidaro with the first initial *P*. It wasn't her father in 519. It was just some other sick person who happened to share his last name.

Harley slumped again the wall. All of a sudden she felt very, very tired. It had been a terribly long day, and the previous night had been sleepless. Her first thought was simply to leave. She could get out of the building, jump back on her bike, and go find the nearest motel. Surely Cain would agree that Harley had kept her side of the bargain.

She took one step toward the elevator and paused. What if it really was her father in the room? Hospitals weren't immune to mistakes. In fact, hospitals were famous for making mistakes. The idea that someone would put the wrong initial on a chart was terribly minor compared to some of the horror stories Harley had heard about people being given the wrong drugs or suffering through the wrong operation. With a flicker of new hope she turned back and pushed open the door.

Stepping into room 519 was like stepping into a jungle. A burst of heat and humidity hit Harley in the face as she came through the door, along with a dark, organic smell. Clouds of mist formed where the cooler air from the hallway spilled into the room. The space inside was large, three or four times as big as any hospital room Harley had seen in the past. But the reason for the space was obvious: The room was packed from wall to wall with strange machines and equipment that none of those other hospitals would have recognized.

Vinelike cables swarmed over the floor, the walls, and even the ceiling. Some of the cables were dark and dull, and some had the flat gleam of ceramic. Still others were bright and shiny, like polished silver or brass. Lights blinked along their surfaces in a rapid, irregular pulse. The cables ranged from wires as fine as hairs to twisted ropes thicker than Harley's arm. In the center of the room the cables fell so densely that they divided the space in two like a beaded curtain.

Other things hung among the mass of cables. Black boxes studded with hundreds of tiny mushroom-shaped buttons dangled from the ceiling like a crop of ripe computer fruit. Metallic stalks shot upward from the floor to end in polished mirror-bright spheres. Streamers of fog drifted through the tangled mass, condensing into drops of water that ran down the cables and dripped onto the floor. The floor absorbed the water with an audible sigh.

Near the front of the room, the elements of the technological rain forest merged into a twisted, lumpy mass the size of coffin. It was several seconds before Harley realized that there was a woman embedded in the twisted mass.

The cables covered her from the neck down and

crept across the top of her head. Button boxes and mirror stalks clustered around her legs. Only her face and one limp hand were free from the covering of technology. Her skin was the purple and yellow of a old bruise.

Harley advanced toward the imprisoned woman with a sick feeling in her stomach. It seemed impossible that someone could be alive within all this wiring and metal, but she knew with awful certainty that this woman was not dead. As she leaned over the still face, the woman's eyes suddenly flew open.

"A natural!" cried the woman. Her voice was surprisingly strong and clear.

Harley took a step back. "What?" Her own voice trembled.

The woman's eyes were a gray so pale they were almost white. They shifted to follow Harley as she retreated. "Oh, they'll be glad to see *you*," said the woman. "Naturals are always in short supply. Never enough."

"Who . . . who are you?" asked Harley.

"I'm the best," the woman replied with obvious pride. "No one lasted as long as me. Two shifts. *Two.*" Her one visible hand tightened into a trembling fist. "No one else managed that."

"That's great," Harley said uncertainly. "Is your name Davisidaro?"

The pupils of the woman's pale eyes shrank

down to tiny pinpoints, then expanded until her whole eye looked black. Her bruised face did not look old, but those black eyes were ancient— ageless.

Harley felt a sudden sharp pain in her temple, followed by a strange tickle that seemed to come from the inside of her head.

"Ahhhh," breathed the woman. "Not *my* name, but *yours.*"

Harley raised a hand to her aching head. "You know me?"

The woman's eyes changed again, her pupils dilating and contracting like a camera lens adjusting to changing light. Another bolt of pain raced through Harley's head, stronger than before.

"I know your father," said the woman. "And he knows me."

"Is he here?" asked Harley. She felt dizzy and disoriented. The tickle in her skull was back.

"If *you* don't know, *I* don't know." The woman waved her fingers toward the door. "I see too much, they say. That's why they keep me in here, so I can't see."

Harley fought to understand. "So you can't see what?"

"What they're thinking. What they're doing." The woman closed her eyes. "They're going to be surprised," she said, her voice dropping to a whisper. "I'm learning to see past all their traps."

For several seconds the woman lay still. Harley was afraid she had fallen asleep, but then the pale eyes snapped open again. "I can see *you* clearly enough," she said. "I can look right *through* you."

The pain in Harley's skull flared into white-hot agony. She stumbled back from the tangled mass of metal and flesh. Harley didn't know how, but she was certain that somehow this woman was responsible for the pain.

"Stop," Harley begged. "Please." The pain eased.

"You don't know anything," the woman said. She let out a loud sigh. "How disappointing."

Harley leaned against the wall and held her throbbing head in her hands. "I'm sorry to disturb you," she said. "I think I should go now."

"Go? *Go?*" The woman laughed. "You can't come all this way and then *go* without stopping in to say hello to your *family.*"

"I thought you said you didn't know where my father was," said Harley. She straightened and walked closer to the woman. "Do you know something?"

The woman's bruised face turned up in an awful mockery of a smile. "I know *everything,*" she said. "Take a look over there." She cut her eyes toward the wall of cables that divided the room.

Harley walked carefully across the room, stepping between the dangling wires and around the obstacles on the floor. As the other half of the room became visible, Harley saw what appeared to be a huge glass cylinder filled with some translucent yellow fluid. In that fluid floated the figure of a second woman.

She was naked. Long straight hair drifted around her head in a cloud. The fluid distorted her color and made it hard to make out details. She was tall but slender, with long legs and a narrow waist. She might have been anywhere between twenty-five and forty. Half her face was hidden behind a mask that was connected to a curving tube.

But what was visible of the woman's face seemed very familiar to Harley. She saw a face very much like it in the mirror every morning.

She remembered then that she *did* know someone named Davisidaro whose first name started with a *P*. Paulina Davisidaro. But that name was attached to a woman dead for almost twelve years.

Harley walked across the room and put her hand on the cool glass of the tube.

"Mother?" she whispered.

Noah pressed his face to the cabin's window and peered out into the darkness. Distant lights glimmered on the surface of the lake, leaving faint silver trails on the smooth water. Other than that, the surrounding woods were as black as the shadow man.

"We should get out of here," Noah said. "We need to put more distance between ourselves and that thing."

Billie walked out of the shadows and stood beside him. "I'm not sure it can find us," she said.

Noah kept his eyes on the darkness. "It found us well enough back at the restaurant."

"Yeah," Billie admitted, "but Legion knew I got away from them while I was in Stone Harbor. That restaurant was close to town. Maybe it was just a coincidence that the dark one found us there."

"Maybe," Noah replied. "But I'm starting to think there's no such thing as coincidence." He flexed his right hand. The skin on his fingers had developed ugly black patches, and there was still an ache when he touched anything. He didn't think he was going to lose any fingers, but he definitely didn't want to try fighting one of those shadow people again with nothing more than a knife. Noah looked over his shoulder at the ladder leading up to the loft. "Did Harley leave anything here besides clothes?" he asked.

"Like what?" said Billie.

"Like a gun."

Billie shook her head quickly. "No. I never saw anything like that. Did Harley have a gun?"

Noah nodded. "A pistol. She found it with her father's things after he disappeared."

"Was her father some kind of soldier?"

"No. A scientist, I think. Or some kind of engineer."

"But he did work for Unit Seventeen," said Billie.

"Yes," Noah answered with another nod. "I mean, *no*. He worked at their base. But like I said before, he wasn't really part of Unit Seventeen."

"Okay," said Billie. "I guess—" She stopped in midsentence.

Noah looked down. "You guess what?"

Billie shook her head. "Never mind." She looked up at Noah. "Maybe we should turn off the lights," she said. "It could make the cabin harder to find."

"The lights?" Noah was surprised at the suggestion. He stared at Billie's face, but he saw no hint of any hidden motive. "Sure," he said at last. "I guess we can turn them off. I don't know if it'll work, but I'm willing to give it a try." Noah joined Billie in walking around the cabin, switching off the lights. A few seconds later the cabin was in complete darkness.

"Noah?" Billie called. "Where are you?"

"Over here." Noah took a step toward the sound of Billie's voice and struck his leg painfully against a low table. Then he stepped on something small and stumbled three steps before falling onto the couch.

"Noah?"

He sat up with a groan. "I'm over here."

A moment later he could feel Billie drawing closer. Even without hearing the soft sound of her clothing in the darkness, he could feel her warmth in the cool room. She had a slight spicy odor that Noah hadn't noticed before—not as strong as a perfume, but nice.

Billie's hand brushed against Noah's face. "Noah? I sure hope that's you."

"It's me." Noah reached up with his undamaged left hand and caught her fingers. "You'd better sit down until your eyes get adapted. I almost broke my neck just getting to the couch."

"I heard you." Billie settled into the cushions at his side. "Are you hurt?"

"No," he replied. "I'm fine. But I still think the best thing would be for us to get out of here." A thought came to mind, and he snapped the fingers of his right hand. Then he winced. Snapping frost-bitten fingers was not a great idea. "I know," he said.

"What?"

"We can call Dee's father."

"Does he know about Legion?" Billie asked.

"A little," Noah told her. "But Mr. Janes is the police chief for Stone Harbor. He can protect us from those shadow things."

Billie's fingers tightened on Noah's. "I don't want to do that," she said.

"Why not?"

"You're the one who told me Legion owned the police," said the red-haired girl. "You said that anything the police or FBI heard went straight to Legion headquarters."

Noah frowned in the darkness. He wished he still knew all the things that he used to know. According to Billie, Noah had once known all about Legion. Now he knew next to nothing. He tried his best to recall his dreams, to find any scrap of memory about seeing Billie in that awful place. But he could conjure up nothing.

"I don't remember saying those things," he admitted. "But anyway, Mr. Janes isn't like that. Unit Seventeen has been trying to find Harley for weeks. They've put out all these bulletins and posters. Mr. Janes has done his best to keep anyone from finding her."

"Let's wait," said Billie. She shifted closer on the couch. Her leg pressed against Noah's, and her soft hair brushed against his cheek.

Noah felt a moment of dizziness and disorientation. "May—Maybe we should go," he stuttered.

"Can't we stay here and see what happens?" Billie asked softly. "I'll feel safer if no one knows about me. No one but *you*, Noah."

The dizziness passed, and Noah's eyes adjusted just enough to make out her outline in the dark room. "I guess we could stay here," he agreed.

"You'll stay all night, right?" Billie asked.

"Sure," said Noah. A warmth was rising in him that overwhelmed his fears. "After what we saw tonight, there's no way I'm going to leave you alone."

Billie raised her face toward Noah's. "I haven't thanked you," she said.

Noah laughed nervously. "For what? Running into you?"

"That was an accident," said Billie. "This isn't." She put a hand behind Noah's head and drew him down. Her lips pressed hard against his mouth.

For a moment Noah had a flash of guilt. An image of Harley's face, with its great dark eyes and smooth olive skin, seemed to float in front of him.

But Billie's hands were insistent, and the taste of her lips was unbelievable. The temperature in the chilly cabin seemed to climb ten degrees as Noah moved his hands to Billie's back and pressed her body against his.

Billie gave a soft sigh. She pulled her lips away from Noah's mouth and brought them close to his ear. "I've been waiting for this for so long," she whispered. "We could never do anything while those monsters were watching us. Now we're alone, we can do anything we want."

Noah found it hard to talk. His breath came in tortured gasps as he kissed Billie's soft neck, and her bare shoulders, and her fingers. Even in the darkness, he imagined he could see the color of her incredible eyes.

She pushed him away for a moment. Then she grabbed him and pulled him back against her. Noah's arms slipped easily around her slim body.

We're alike, Billie said. This time her voice sounded in Noah's mind instead of his ears. Her voice was much stronger there, as powerful and clear as a trumpet blast.

"Alike," Noah whispered in response.

Billie kissed Noah at the curve of his jaw. Then on his cheek. Then on his lips. *We were tortured together and tested together. But we're stronger than them.* Even during the kiss, the mind voice didn't falter. *Now we'll always be together.*

Noah hugged her to him and kissed her hungrily. "Always." He had never felt anything like this before. There had been plenty of girls at school, but none of them had ever affected him this way. He had to have Billie. He needed Billie more than air.

Love me, said the voice in his mind.

There was a noise from outside the cabin.

Noah froze. Billie was warm against him. His heart was pounding with the need to kiss her again. And to do more. But that one sound over-ruled everything else.

The sound came again. This time it was clearly the breaking of fallen branches, followed by a shuf-fling, dragging sound.

"What is it?" whispered Billie.

Noah slowly moved away from her. "Get ready," he said. "It might just be an animal. But it might not." He stood up and peered into the dark-ness. He needed a weapon. Something longer and more lethal than a kitchen knife.

The sound changed. It was on the porch now. A thump. A pause. And then another thump.

Noah crept toward the fireplace. There was a rack of tools beside the dark opening. Noah picked up the first one and felt along the shaft until he came to a wide, flat blade. A shovel. He put it back on the rack and tried the next tool. This time his fingers found the wicked hook and sharp point of a poker. He weighed the weapon in his hands. It was no gun, but it would have to do.

Billie stood. "Could it be Harley coming back?"

There was another thump outside, then another, like terribly slow steps. The wooden porch beams creaked under some terrible weight.

"No," Noah whispered. "That's not Harley."

The knob on the front door rattled for a moment, then was silent.

Billie moved to Noah's side. "Is there another way out of here?"

"No," said Noah. There was another creak from the porch. It was farther away. "Stay still. It may not know we're in here."

The door creaked. Then the wood bowed inward, groaning and crackling. Planks burst away from the frame, flew across the room, and smashed into the wall.

The rising moon lent a pale light to the night. Against that silver glow, the pure blackness of the shadow man stood in the broken door frame. Its red eyes scanned the room. From the way they quickly locked on Noah and Billie, there was no doubt about the thing's ability to see in the dark.

Noah raised the fireplace poker. "Stay back," he said. He wasn't sure if he meant it as a warning to Billie or to the thing coming through the door. He knew only that he had to protect Billie, no matter what the cost.

The shadow man was again unimpressed. It

walked toward Noah at the same unhurried pace with which it had destroyed the Fiddler's Crab. It pushed aside a lamp, which smashed in a momentary flash of yellow light. A dark hand flicked out, and the couch where Noah and Billie had been kissing only moments before was pushed over onto its back. Frost spread over the cushions.

"Get ready," Noah whispered to Billie. "I don't think I can stop it, but it moves pretty slowly. I'll try to distract it, then we'll both run for the door."

Billie nodded. "Right." She edged to the right.

As soon as she moved, the shadow man turned toward her.

"Hey!" shouted Noah. "Over here!" He stepped between Billie and the dark thing. His injured hand was throbbing, but he raised the poker over his right shoulder and bent his knees. When the shadow took another step forward, Noah swung the poker at the thing's head as if he were trying to hit a home run.

The iron point of the tool vanished into the shadow right below the glowing eyes. For a moment Noah felt resistance, and ice began to spread up the shaft of the poker. Then the makeshift weapon tore free in a gout of cold blue flame.

Liquid darkness poured from the wound and

splashed on the floor like some obscene fluid. The red eyes dimmed to a dull cherry glow.

"Now!" shouted Noah. As Billie ran toward the door Noah hurled the poker into the shadow man. The metal rod went through the shadow thing's chest like a harpoon. More blue flames erupted, and the flow of black ooze leaving the wounds became a flood. Cold mist pooled along the floor of the cabin. The sharp smell of ozone filled the air, and there was a hiss like air escaping from a punctured tire.

Noah leaped past the wounded thing and sprinted around the fallen furniture. Billie was almost at the door when she skidded to a halt and screamed, "There's another one!" She took a step backward, and Noah saw a second shadow man coming through the opening where the door had been.

He turned and looked at the first of the creatures. It was still bleeding darkness, but it had its hands on the poker. As Noah watched, it pulled the weapon free and threw it on the floor. Ice now covered the poker in a jacket two inches thick. Still leaking shadow stuff onto the floor, the wounded creature started toward Noah.

There were no more weapons, no way out, and not much time.

"Noah!" Billie shouted. "The window!"

Noah bent and picked up a chair. "This way!"

he shouted, then he heaved the chair through the front window of the cabin.

The shattering glass seemed as loud as an explosion. Noah kicked away the largest shards that remained in the window frame, then he grabbed Billie's hand and pulled her out onto the porch.

"What do we do?" she asked.

"Run," Noah ordered. "Run for my car."

The full moon had vanished behind clouds, and the trail through the rocks was hard to make out. Here and there Noah spotted footsteps of melting frost where the shadows had passed. From the number of footsteps, it seemed that the creatures had taken many wrong turns and done a lot of backtracking within the rock maze. Either that, or there were more than two of the things.

Billie held onto Noah's fingers as they ran. She was small, and her legs were not as long as Harley's, but she moved her feet quickly. Noah was supposed to be the track star, but by the time they reached the highway, he was the one who was struggling to breathe.

Just down the road, the Mustang waited. Noah sucked in a deep breath and looked back down the path. There was no sign of the shadow men.

"I think we made it," he said.

Billie nodded. She put her arms around Noah's

waist and hugged him with surprising strength. "Thanks to you," she said.

Noah bent his head and gave her a quick kiss. He smiled at her as he straightened. "Come on," he said. "Let's put some miles between us and those things."

Only when he took a step closer to the car did he see what had been done. The Mustang's windshield was covered with a network of fine cracks. The hood of the car was dented. It had been torn free of its hinges and dropped back in place. The front wheels were nothing but bits of rubber lying in the road next to gleaming metal rims. Noah could visualize the shadows applying their infinitely cold touch, turning the rubber as brittle as glass.

But it didn't matter *how* it had been done. All that mattered was that the Mustang wasn't going anywhere.

The woman in the tube opened her eyes.

Harley's breath caught in her throat as the woman's dark gaze turned her way. But the eyes didn't pause. They turned left and right with no pattern, their aim traveling randomly around the room. After a few seconds the eyes closed again. The woman's fingers trembled. Her legs jerked in spasms. Then she was still.

"Mother," Harley whispered again.

It wasn't really possible that this tortured woman was her mother. It couldn't be. Harley had been only a small child, but she remembered going to her mother's funeral. She remembered her father's tears. He had cried that night, and on a hundred other nights, for his lost wife. Harley couldn't even begin to count how many times she had heard the story of her parents' romance, of their wonderful love for each other, and of Paulina's tragic death.

But now Harley was face-to-face, or at least face-to-glass, with a woman who might well be her missing mother. The name was right, and the woman's features were right. But if that was true, then every word of the history that Harley had always believed was a lie.

Harley was struck with a sudden thought. Her father's journal had mentioned a *P* in its first entries. "P agreed to accept enhancement," the note had read. She put her hand to the smooth glass. What if the initial in the journal had been for her mother's name? Could her mother have been involved with the work on "trans-alpha"? Might this "enhancement" have been the real source of the accident that had taken Paulina Davisidaro away?

Harley didn't have enough information. She couldn't be sure about the woman, or the journal, or even the glass tube. It could be the woman's prison, or it could be keeping her alive. She remembered the medical chart on the door of the room.

"Hang on," Harley said to the sleeping woman. "I'll be right back." It was a silly thing to say. The woman in the tube might be Harley's mother, but there was little chance she had any awareness of anything going on outside her liquid chamber.

Before Harley could turn around, she felt a sudden pressure on her back.

"Please don't move, Ms. Davisidaro," said a low voice. "After so much trouble, it would be a shame to kill you."

Harley recognized the voice without seeing the speaker. "Commander Braddock."

"You remember me," said the commander. "That's good." The pressure on her back increased as something small and hard was shoved against her spine. "I trust you have no doubt what I'll do if you don't cooperate."

"No," Harley replied. Braddock had already tried to kill her at least once. Harley had no illusions that he wouldn't do so again at the first excuse.

"I'm glad to see you're being so cooperative," said the commander. "Now, hands up, please."

Harley was tempted to reach for her revolver, but she raised her hands slowly. The pressure disappeared from her back.

Braddock moved around to where she could see him. The stocky man had traded in his garish yellow suit for a Unit 17 uniform of dark blue. In his hand he held what appeared to be a bent tube of metal. There was no trigger that Harley could see, and no opening at the end of the tube. But from the way Braddock held the device, Harley had no doubt it was a weapon.

"Where is my father?" she demanded.

A sneer came to Braddock's face. "You're not in a position to be asking questions," he told her.

Harley began to slowly lower her hands. "All I want to do is see my father," she said. "I don't care about anything else. Let me talk to my dad, and I won't bother you anymore."

Braddock let out a bark of hard laughter. "I can arrange it so that you'll never bother me again," he shot back. "And I don't have to give you a thing."

The woman in the tube suddenly convulsed, striking her bare foot against the side of the glass with a solid thump. Braddock turned toward the sound.

As he did, Harley dropped her hand to the small of her back and came out with the revolver. Quickly she shoved the short-nosed gun into Braddock's ribs. "Drop that thing," she said. "Now."

The commander looked down at the dark pistol. "What an ugly weapon. Where did you come up with that?"

"Never mind," Harley replied. "As long as you know I'll use it."

Braddock opened his hand and let the bent tube drop. It fluttered through the air as it fell, striking the floor as lightly as a falling feather. "Now," he said. "What is it you really want?"

"My father," Harley answered. "Tell me where he is, right now." She pressed her lips into a hard white line. "Tell me, or I'll kill you."

"Will you?" Braddock smiled.

"I'm serious," Harley snarled. She pressed hard

on the gun, hoping that the barrel digging into his ribs would cause Braddock some pain. Her finger tightened on the trigger.

The commander glanced down at Harley's hand. "Yes," he said. "I can see that you are serious."

There was a flash of white light. The world spun around. Colors faded to gray. Something hard and cold came up and slammed Harley in the face.

Katie Davisidaro was three years old. Her daddy sometimes called her "Harley." Katie thought that was really funny.

She lived in a little square house on a tiny military base somewhere on the wide, empty prairies. Today was going to be a happy day. Today was when Mommy and Daddy were taking her to look at a puppy. Katie was very excited about the puppy.

She ran across a lawn of dry brown grass. Mommy caught her under the arms and lifted her up into the sky.

"Are you ready, Katie?" Mommy asked.

Katie nodded and smiled at her mommy.

When Harley awoke, she was sitting in a metal chair in the center of a small, dark room.

Her pistol was gone. So was her jacket. Sharp pain flared down the side of her face. When she tried to stand, she found that there were strips of something binding her wrists and ankles to the chair. The stuff looked like kite string, but no matter how Harley pulled or twisted, the thin straps would not give an inch.

Only seconds after she had awakened, the door opened and three men came in. One of them was Commander Braddock. The other two were younger, but they also were dressed in the featureless blue jumpsuits of Unit 17. One of the guys had a red splotch on his face, like a bad birthmark. The other had black hair cut so short that it was little more than dark stubble on his skull. Both of them of them carried the bent metal tubes in their hands.

"Did you have a nice dream, Ms. Davisidaro?" asked Braddock.

Harley looked down at the floor and didn't answer.

Braddock walked slowly around her. "You know, these guns don't always play so soft. One notch up, and they'll have you in convulsions for an hour. Two notches, and your heart will stop." He snapped his fingers. "Just like that."

"Where's my father?" asked Harley.

The commander snorted. "I am getting so *tired* of that question," he said. "If you ask again, I will show you just how unpleasant an hour-long seizure can be. Do you understand?"

Harley was silent.

"Do you understand?" shouted Braddock.

"Yes," Harley replied.

"Good." Braddock stopped his pacing. "If you want to avoid pain, I suggest you find a new topic for discussion."

Harley looked up at him. Her hair had fallen across her face. With both hands bound, she couldn't push it away. "That woman up there," she said through her screen of hair. "Is she my mother?"

"Well," said Braddock, "at least that's a new question. I'm not going to answer it, but it is new." He turned and nodded to the man with the splotched face. The man whirled around and marched sharply out of the room.

Braddock turned back to Harley. "Now, here's how this is going to work. I'm going to ask some very simple questions, and you're going to answer them, understand?" Harley gave no reply, but this time Braddock went right on talking. "First we want to know about your companion."

"What companion?"

Braddock leaned down and jabbed a finger an inch away from Harley's nose. "I'm not an idiot," he growled, "and I don't believe you are, either. I may be wrong. But it won't matter. Idiot or not, you're still going to tell me everything I want to know."

The door opened, and the man with the red

mark returned. In his hands was a silvery metal box a little bigger than a shoe box.

"Ah," said Braddock. He walked over to the man and opened the box. He lifted out an ugly gray device. It looked a bit like a blow dryer, but this blow dryer had been half melted, merged with a screwdriver and a dentist's drill, then frozen with all three implements jutting out at different angles. Deep green lights pulsed along its sides.

"Now," Braddock said as he brought the thing over to Harley. "Who is your companion?"

Harley shook her head. "I don't—"

The commander pressed the blunt snout of the device against Harley's forehead. The room vanished in a wave of white-hot misery.

Harley would have sworn she had known pain. She had broken her leg in a motorcycle accident. She'd had burns, scrapes, cuts, and illnesses. But what she'd felt from those things—even all those things put together—couldn't possibly compare to what she felt now.

Red agony soared over her. She wanted to scream, but she couldn't move. The pain had swallowed up all sight and sound, all sense of her body, drowning her in endless boiling lava of pure suffering.

And then it was gone as instantly as it had begun.

Harley gasped. She was back in the little room

with Commander Braddock and the two Unit 17 soldiers. Her skin tingled and her muscles twitched with the memory of the pain. The soldier with the short haircut was laughing in a high, squeaky giggle.

Braddock pulled back the ugly dryer-device and leaned over her. A smile turned up the ends of his thin gray mustache. "You see," he said softly. "You'll tell me exactly what I want to know. Won't you?"

"Yes," gasped Harley. "Anything." She didn't know what it was that Braddock wanted to find out, but she would have talked for hours just to keep that pain from coming back.

The commander nodded. "Before we chat further, I want to demonstrate the full range of this little toy." He moved the device toward Harley's leg.

"No!" shouted Harley. "Don't! I'll tell you what you want to know."

"Shhh," Braddock whispered, almost gently. He tapped a blunt finger against his mouth. "No pain this time. You'll see."

Instead of pressing the blunt opening of the device to Harley's leg, he tapped her on the left thigh with one of the sharper, needlelike points. Braddock had told the truth—there was no pain. Instead Harley felt a momentary tingling along the length of her left leg, as though it had fallen asleep.

When the tingling passed, there was no feeling in her leg. No feeling at all.

The soldier with the crew cut began to giggle again. "That's real good, sir."

Braddock waved him into silence. "Be quiet, Corporal."

Harley tried to move her toes or press her leg against its restraints. Nothing. She couldn't move her left leg. She couldn't even feel her left leg. She stared down in distress. "What have you done?"

Braddock tapped Harley with the needlelike point on the right side. The tingling came again. Now both her legs were as still and unfeeling as wood.

The commander looked up. "It's permanent, you know."

Acid rose in Harley's throat. "What?" she choked out.

"Permanent." The commander nodded. He straightened. "I understand you were something of a track star. Well, those days are past. You'll never stand on your own feet again. Never run. Never feel the least sensation from your waist down."

Panic started Harley's heart racing. Her breath came fast and shallow. "Can't you fix it?" she asked.

"Oh, yes," mused Braddock. "I suppose I could." He turned the ugly device over in his hands. "Or I could use it on your arms."

"No!" cried Harley.

"Yes," said Braddock. "And I think on your mouth. On the rest of your body. Even on your eyes." He traced one finger along the side of the gleaming needle. "How would you like that?"

"No," Harley said again. Tears had begun to well up in her eyes. She strained with everything she had to move her legs. Harley had broken the record for the mile at three different schools, but no matter how she struggled, she couldn't get even a quiver out of her lower limbs. Her legs were dead.

"Then," continued Braddock, his voice becoming more scornful with each word, "once you're nothing more than a motionless, blind little sack of maggot meat"—he spit the words into Harley's face—"*then* we'll try the pain again. What do you think?"

Harley let her chin drop down. Tears rolled down her face and dripped into her lap. She felt so ashamed.

She had always considered herself to be tough. She wouldn't be bullied. She could stand up for herself. She did *not* cry. But Braddock had brought her to tears in a matter of minutes.

"I'll tell you anything," she said through her tears.

"Of course you will," said Braddock. His voice settled into a tone of fake kindness that made Harley want to curl into a ball and hide. He touched the device to Harley's legs again, and the feeling returned. Her legs hurt as though they had been beaten by a baseball bat. It was the most wonderful thing that Harley had ever felt.

Braddock crouched down in front of her. "I asked you before if you understood what I was capable of," he said. "You thought you knew then. Now you really know."

"Yes," said Harley. She sniffed and blinked the tears away from her eyes.

"Fine." The commander stood up straight. He took the ugly device and returned it to its metal box, then began to pace around the room again. "You know, you had us all fooled."

"I did?"

Braddock nodded. "You were under such close observation, we never thought that you would be recruited."

"Recruited?" Harley asked, feeling bewildered.

"Come now," said the commander. "We know you had help. You disabled a very complex security system back at Tulley Hill. You don't have the knowledge or equipment to do that by yourself. Just to get into this room tonight, you had to bypass a thousand safety checks." He stopped in front of Harley. "Do you deny you had help?"

Cain. Harley remembered how Cain had provided the security pass that had allowed her to move freely around the Tulley Hill facility. He had to have done something here to allow Harley to enter. "I . . . I had help," she admitted.

"Very good," said Braddock. "Now, we also know that you were with another person when you were captured at Tulley Hill. We had two agents who were prepared to name your companion." He put one beefy hand on Harley's shoulder. "Unfortunately, both those agents were lost in the line of duty."

"I'm sorry," Harley told him. The agents that Braddock was talking about had to be Caroline Crewson, who had pretended to be Noah's girlfriend, and the fake track coach, Rocklin. Both of them had turned out to be Unit 17 agents, and both of them had known about Noah. But it seemed that neither of them had survived long enough to tell what they had learned.

"No, you're not sorry," said Braddock. "But that's all right. They'll soon be avenged." His fingers dug into the flesh at Harley's shoulder. "Now. Tell me the name of your companion."

The memory of the pain was still fresh in Harley's mind, and the thought of the terrible deadness in her legs made Harley's stomach feel like water. Noah's name came to her lips. But at the last moment she thought of another name. The perfect name.

"Josh," she said. "His name was Josh McQuinn."

Josh McQuinn had been in high school with Noah. He had been Noah's closest friend for years, but he had turned out to be an agent of Legion, assigned to watch over Noah. As far as Harley knew, none of the people in Unit 17 was aware of him. He was also quite conveniently dead.

"Josh McQuinn," repeated the commander. "And was this McQuinn an agent of Umbra?"

"Umbra?" Harley shook her head. "I don't know what that is."

"What about Legion?"

"Yes," Harley agreed with a nod. "He worked for Legion."

Braddock smiled his cold smile. "See, now we're getting somewhere." He turned and looked at the man with the splotched face. "Well, Sergeant Baines. What are our results?"

The man reached into the metal box. This time he came out with something about the size and shape of a deck of cards. It looked for all the world like a small piece of clear plastic embedded with tiny colored Christmas lights. "Half and half," said the man. His voice was hoarse and rasping. "This McQuinn is real, and he worked for Legion. But that's not the name of the person who helped her."

Braddock spun around and looked at Harley. "You lied to me," he hissed.

"I—"

"You lied!" Braddock's voice rose into a

thundering shout. "Which will it be? Pain or paralysis?"

Harley shivered. "I'll tell the truth."

The commander shook his head. "It's too late for that now." He went back to the box and drew out the torture gun. "I think I'll simply kill one finger on your left hand. Every time you lie to me, I'll kill another. And this time I'll *leave* them dead. What do you think?"

"Don't," Harley said. She gritted her teeth.

The soldier with the stubbly hair began to giggle again.

Braddock started toward her. "It won't hurt," he said softly. "In fact, it'll never hurt again."

Harley balled her hand into a fist as Braddock leaned over her. "I'll tell!" she screamed.

"Be careful," Braddock warned. He lowered the sharp point of the device to within a few inches of Harley's hand. "If I slip, you might lose your whole arm instead of just a finger."

Harley looked up at the ceiling. She didn't want to watch as Braddock took parts of her body away.

The ground shook under her. Vibrations ran through her body. Harley frowned. It felt different this time.

When she glanced down, Braddock and the other two soldiers were looking toward the door. The shaking came again. This time there was a muffled thump against the door. Harley felt her ears pop.

"Agran! Baines!" Braddock barked. "Get out there and see what's going on."

The two soldiers nodded. The man with the splotched face put the metal box down on the floor. Holding their weapons at the ready, the two men walked out the door. A moment later there was a sharp cracking sound. Then silence.

The commander took a step toward the door. "Baines?" he called. "Agran? What's going on?"

The door flew open, and Cain stepped into the room.

The agent still wore his trench coat and suit, but now his clothes were torn. Blood dribbled down the side of his long face and stained the shoulder of his coat. In his hand was what appeared to be his black ballpoint pen.

Commander Braddock's face turned red with rage. "You!" he snarled.

"Me," said Cain. He pointed the pen at Braddock. Blue-white lightning arced from the point of the pen and struck the stocky commander in the chest. Braddock's back arched as twisting bolts of electricity ran over his body. Smoke rose from the torture gun still clutched in his fingers.

When the lightning stopped, Braddock fell to the floor.

"Is he dead?" Harley asked.

Cain dropped the pen into the pocket of his

trench coat. "I don't know." He stepped over the commander's body and walked around to the back of Harley's chair. There was a soft pop, and the bonds holding her hands and feet vanished.

"Let's move," said Cain. He started out the door. "They'll have a truckload of soldiers down here any minute, and that's more than I can handle."

Harley got to her feet and staggered after him. Her legs still hurt, but it sure beat the alternative.

The clean, neat hallway of the hidden hospital was now filled with smoke, rubble, and broken glass. "What did you do?" asked Harley as they squeezed through a twisted door.

"I was in a hurry," said Cain. "There was no time to be subtle."

They passed through a final door and stepped out into the cold Connecticut night. Two or three inches of thick, white snow were already on the ground, and more was falling.

When they reached the empty parking lot, Cain turned around quickly. "Are you injured?" he asked.

Harley shook her head. "You look like the one who's injured. You're bleeding pretty badly."

Cain lifted a hand and dabbed at his cheek. "It's not my blood," he said.

"How did you know where I was?" asked Harley.

"I didn't know for sure until I saw you," said Cain. "Come on. We need to get away from here before Unit Seventeen shows up with a few helicopters and tanks." He walked away rapidly, the heels of his shoes crunching in the snow.

Harley followed him across the parking lot. "Wait!" she called. "What about my father?"

"He's not here."

"Then what about my mother?"

Cain stopped. "What about her?" he asked.

Harley caught up with the agent and tugged on his coat until he stopped walking. She moved around him until she could look up at his long face. "Is that woman in there my mother?"

After a moment's hesitation, Cain nodded. "I can't be certain. But that seems to be the case."

"How can that be?" Harley cried. "My mother is dead!"

Cain frowned. "Look. We will talk again. But not here. Not now. I have other emergencies to take care of, and you have to get back to Stone Harbor right away."

"Why?"

"Because I've made a serious mistake," replied Cain. "More than one, actually. I should never have allowed you to get trapped in this place. The other mistake was with Noah. I badly underestimated the danger of his situation. If you don't go to his aid immediately, he'll almost certainly die."

The words jarred Harley. "Has Legion found him? Or Unit Seventeen?"

Cain shook his head. "Just get back there and help," he said. "I'll be along as soon as I possibly can." He reached into his pocket and pulled out the lightning pen. "Here. Take this."

Harley accepted the little weapon gingerly. "How does it work?"

"Press both buttons at the same time," said Cain. "And by the way, I would highly recommend against putting it in a snug pocket." With that Cain turned and began to run away into the night.

"Thank you," Harley shouted after him. "Thanks for saving me."

Cain's voice drifted back out of the darkness. "Don't thank me! It was my fault. Go save Noah." When the words ended, he was gone.

Harley hurried to the bushes where she had left her motorcycle and her backpack. But when she arrived there, she found nothing. The two thousand dollars Cain had loaned her were gone. The Sportster, which she had loved and cared for since she was too young to drive it, had been taken as well. Worst of all, she had again lost the journal that was her only link with her father.

She shivered in the cold wind. She had to do something. If she stayed here, she would either freeze to death or be captured by Unit 17. One idea seemed about as unpleasant as the other.

Harley ran up the street, grateful that her legs were still capable of running. It was very late, almost dawn. All the small stores along the road were closed. But two blocks away, traffic still ran along the interstate. If she was going to find any help, she would find it there.

She climbed the slippery, snow-covered grass at the side of the road and stumbled out onto the shoulder. Even here, traffic was reduced to a line of widely separated vehicles. From a quarter mile away, Harley spotted the single headlight of an approaching motorcycle. She stepped out onto the roadway, waving her hands wildly over her head.

The motorcycle had to swerve to miss her, but it stopped. When she saw that it was an old Harley-Davidson flathead, she knew things were going to work out after all.

"You trying to get yourself killed, girl?" said the man on the bike. He was a big man, not just in height, but in bulk. Harley would have bet he weighed over three hundred pounds, and not much of that was fat. His muscle-corded forearms were as thick as her neck.

"It's an emergency," said Harley.

"Yeah?" The man rolled the bike over to the side of the road and looked her up and down. A wide grin came to his face. "What's wrong, baby? You need something?"

Harley took out the pen Cain had given her. "I need your bike," she said.

The biker laughed. "Yeah, sure. You want my jacket, too?"

"Yes," said Harley. "And your billfold."

The man threw back his head and laughed. "You're crazy, girl. Now, you want to hop on here or not?" He patted the leather seat behind him. "I've got it warmed up just for you."

Harley pointed the pen at the ground at the side of the interstate and pressed both buttons. The bolt of lightning that sprang out ripped into the ground. A miniature clap of thunder boomed as both the snow and the grass were burned away, leaving a hole three feet across.

"I want the bike," Harley repeated. "And the jacket. And your wallet." She pointed the pen toward the biker.

The man was off the motorcycle in a second. He peeled off his black leather jacket and tossed it on the seat, then followed it with a billfold that was decorated by a length of chain. "You need anything else?" he asked. There was no "girl" or "baby" added this time.

"Move away," Harley instructed. As the man stepped back from the bike, she picked up the jacket and slid it on. It was enormous on her, but it was also deliciously warm. She reached into the billfold, drew out a pair of bills, and tossed them on the ground.

"Here," she said. "Go call someone."

The biker nodded. His eyes were wide and frightened. "What are you?"

"Someone in a hurry," said Harley. She cranked up the motorcycle. "I'll call you and tell you where to find the bike," she shouted over the roar of the motor. "Thanks for the loan!"

With that she spun around and started for Stone Harbor.

Noah reached into the waterfall and brought a handful of water to his lips. The water was clear, and so cold that it made his fingers and his teeth ache. But it sure tasted good.

A warm front had come through during the night, bringing with it air that felt more like early September than the end of November. Still, a rim of ice lingered along the pool at the bottom of the waterfall. More ice clung to the rocks as Noah scrambled along the stony trail. He walked slowly. As tired as he was, Noah didn't feel too steady—and the slippery footing only made it worse. The last thing he wanted to do was take a dip in the freezing stream beside the trail.

He squeezed into the dark gap between a pair of sandstone boulders and trudged up a short slope. A cliff of rugged, weathered stone rose sixty feet above the stream. At its base was a sheltered area, a pocket in the cliff wall that was ten feet wide and twice as deep. The cave had a six-foot ceiling, and Noah had to duck as he entered the tiny space, but the place had served as much-needed shelter during the night.

Billie was still stretched out on the sandy floor, with Noah's jacket spread over her like a blanket. Her eyes popped open as Noah approached. "Good morning," she said. She took a deep breath and sat up.

"Good morning to you." He sat down on the ground beside her. "There's water out there if you want it."

"What about the dark ones?" Billie asked.

Noah shook his head. "No sign of them."

The red-haired girl put her hands over her head and stretched, bending her back like a cat. "That's wonderful," she breathed. She looked around at the little cave. "I can easily believe they didn't find this place. I'm just amazed that *you* found it."

"You should be glad I was in Scouts," he said. "They brought us up here to show us some old Indian sites." He reached over and ran his hand down the rough stone wall. "I don't think they expected any of us to move in, though."

Billie stood up and brushed loose sand from her sweater and skirt. She ran her fingers through her hair and made a face. "I must look awful."

"Are you kidding?" said Noah. "You look great."

Billie smiled at him. "Thanks." She handed over Noah's jacket. "I'm glad it decided to warm up before we froze to death. But now what are we going to do?"

Noah shrugged. "We could try to go back to

the cabin. Those things could be gone by now."

"Or they could be waiting for us." Billie shook her head. "Next idea, please."

"There's that store that you walked to the other day," Noah suggested. "It's not too far from here. It's still early, but by the time we get there they'll be open. From there we can try to get a ride back to town."

"All right," said Billie. "Let's go." She stepped past Noah and walked out into the sunshine.

Noah stood, bumped his head on the low roof, then crouched and followed her.

The sun was bright for the first hour as they walked through the woods. With the lake sparkling off to the right, birds fluttering through the trees, and Billie at his side, Noah felt more as though he were going on a picnic than fleeing for his life.

"Who are you going to call?" Billie asked suddenly.

"What?"

"When we get to the store. Who are you going to call?"

Noah shrugged. "Dee's father, I guess. He's the only one who can give us any kind of protection."

"The police chief?" Billie frowned. "Can't we go to someone else?"

"I guess we could just call Dee."

"There's no one else?"

"Nobody I can think of," said Noah. "I can't exactly go to my parents with this."

Billie stopped walking and leaned back against a tree. "What about your friends from the Internet?" she suggested.

Noah shook his head. "I don't even know who they are. Or *where* they are. They might not even be in this country."

"There must be someone else in Stone Harbor who knows what's going on," Billie insisted.

"Not really," said Noah. "There was just me and Harley to begin with. We told Dee and her dad a little. That's it."

Billie reached out and took Noah's hands. With a gentle tug, she drew him close. "You have to trust me," she said softly.

Noah wasn't sure what to say. "I do trust you."

"But you're not telling me everything," said Billie. "I know you're not." Her fingers slipped up into Noah's hair. She pulled his face down to hers, her lips brushing against his cheek. "Tell me who else is involved," she whispered.

Noah again felt a burst of the powerful attraction that had overcome him the night before. But this time it was mixed with confusion and more than a little fear—emotions that had sprung up out of nowhere. "I've told you everything I know."

"You were a product of a Legion breeding

program," said Billie. She lowered her face and kissed Noah on the neck. "Is that right?"

Noah closed his eyes. "Yes," he said, momentarily giving in to a warm sensation rushing up his spine. "At least that's what Josh told me."

"And this Josh was the one who watched over you for Legion?"

"Yes."

"And he's dead."

"Yes," gasped Noah. He felt intense waves of pleasure as Billie stroked her fingers across the side of his face.

Billie's voice was only a faint whisper, but her questions carried more force than a shout. "Harley was not involved with Legion."

"No," said Noah. His knees trembled. "I told you. Her father was kidnapped by Unit Seventeen."

"And the others you talked about. This old girlfriend of yours and the track coach." Billie's lips ran along the top of Noah's ear. "Are you sure they're dead?"

"I . . . I'm not sure," Noah murmured. "No one has seen them since the facility was closed."

Billie's hands went around his back, pulling him down. Noah stumbled and fell to his knees. "There's someone else," she said in her insistent whisper. "Someone you're not telling me about."

Noah shook his head, trying to clear it. "No. That's all."

"It's not," said Billie. "Who else is involved?" She jerked his head up and kissed him hard on the lips. "Tell me, Noah!"

A name and face flashed into Noah's mind. "You're right," he coughed out. "There is someone."

"Who?" demanded Billie. "Who is it?"

"He calls himself Cain."

Billie pushed Noah away with such force that he fell on the ground. "Cain!" she shouted. "He's here?" She looked around wildly, as if she expected the agent to step out of the trees.

Noah's head swam. He felt as if his thoughts had been packed in cotton. He rolled over, getting to his hands and knees. "What did you do to me?" He tried to stand, but he was too dizzy. With his face toward the ground, Noah saw Billie's smooth legs approaching.

"I did nothing that you didn't want me to do," she said. Her voice dripped sarcasm. "Didn't you want someone to talk to? Someone small and powerless, someone you could help?" Billie's delicate foot came up, driving her toe into Noah's stomach with astounding strength.

The air was forced from Noah's lungs in a painful rush. He fell facedown on the ground. As a second kick smashed into his ribs, Noah curled into a ball. He tried to draw in a breath, but the best he could manage were a few agonizing sips of air.

"I had such big hopes for you," Billie spat. "Do you have any idea how long we worked to infiltrate the Legion breeding program?" She began to pace around Noah as he rolled on the ground. "In ten years of searching, yours was the only name we found. We were counting on your connections to uncover the whole system. But now all we have is you and the daughter of some Unit Seventeen scientist."

Noah pulled in a single rasping breath. "Leave Harley alone," he croaked.

Billie blinked, and her face took on a frighteningly real expression of innocence. "Oh, Noah," she said. "You can't mean you care more for Harley than you do for me." She blinked her turquoise eyes.

Despite what had just happened, Noah felt a surge of emotion. He had a sudden desire to get up from the ground and hold Billie. He had to show her he cared about her. He held up his arms. "Billie," he sighed.

Laughter washed over him. *You really are an idiot,* said a diamond-hard voice inside his head. *Legion labored ten generations, and look what they have to show for it. Your latent talents do nothing but leave you wide open to every form of mental suggestion.*

"Who are you?" gasped Noah. His breathing was still painful, but the cobwebs in his head were beginning to clear. Noah rolled onto his knees and started to get up.

"Whoever you want me to be," Billie said in a sweet voice. "Your poor little broken angel."

Noah put one hand against a tree for support and stood, swaying, on his feet. "*Fallen* angel is more like it," he said.

Billie smiled. "Oh, that's very clever. I'll have to remember that."

There was a crackle of branches from the woods behind her. A figure of darkness appeared. The shadow man pushed its way past the trees. Even in the warm sunshine, it was so black that it seemed to have no depth. It was as if someone had taken a pair of scissors and cut a hole in the world in the shape of a man.

Despite what had just happened, Noah felt a surge of fear as the dark one approached Billie. "Look out!" he shouted. He pushed himself away from the tree and searched the ground for a branch or stone that could serve as a weapon.

Billie glanced over her shoulder casually. "It's about time you got here," she said to the shadow. "I've just about had enough of walking around in these filthy woods."

"Sorry," said the shadow. Its voice was terribly deep and hollow, like a man talking from the bottom of a well.

Noah looked on in shock as the towering dark

figure stopped beside the small girl. Billie turned back to Noah and smiled.

"Surprise!" she said brightly. "As it turns out, you would have told me anything." She ran her hands slowly down her arms. "Just to please me. But we didn't know that when we were planning this little escape." She reached out and actually stroked the side of the shadow thing. White frost spread over Billie's hand and up her arm, but she didn't seem to mind.

A terrible certainty came over Noah. "You brought the shadows in to chase us, so you could get me to confide in you."

"And it worked," replied Billie. "Though if they had left me alone for a few more minutes last night, there would have been no reason for me to spend the night on a cold dirt floor." She looked up at the black thing beside her. There was a fire in the girl's blue-green eyes that more than matched the red glow from the dark one's. "Another ten minutes alone in that cabin, and he would have handed me the Unit Seventeen girl's skull for a keepsake. But you bumblers had to interrupt us."

"Sorry," the creature repeated in its slow, hollow voice. "We followed the times we were told."

Billie put her hands on her hips. "Next time show a little more flexibility," she said.

There was the sound of movement behind

Noah. He turned and saw a second shadow creature approaching along the shore of the lake. Then
he spotted a third walking along the other side of
the stream.

"How many of these things are there?" Noah
asked.

Billie clicked her tongue. "Now, now, now.
Haven't you ever watched one of those old spy pictures? It's a terrible idea to tell the enemy the size
of your forces."

Noah stared into her spellbinding eyes. "Am I
your enemy?"

"Yes," Billie replied. "Whether you know it or
not, you are Legion. That makes you the enemy of
Umbra."

The word rang some distant bell in Noah's
memory, something to do with space or an eclipse.
"What's Umbra?"

Billie shook her head. "I have no reason to ex-
plain myself to you." She turned to the shadow at
her side. "Take him back to the cabin. He knows
little, but he may still know where to find the Unit
Seventeen girl."

Until that moment Noah's overwhelming feeling had been one of confusion, but now a terrible
sense of betrayal began to rise, and with it, a white-
hot rage. "If you're talking about Harley," he said,
"I don't know where she is. Even if I did, I'd never
tell you."

Billie pushed her lips out into a pout. "Now, honey. You know you would. All I have to do is ask you nicely." She tilted her head to the side and smiled.

A shock of desire ran through Noah, followed by despair and guilt. He knew that Billie's power was far more than just normal attraction, but he was still ashamed at the ease with which she could twist his mind. "You can't have Harley," he said through gritted teeth. "You'll never find her."

"Oh, we'll find her," said Billie. "With you to provide an entry into Legion, and Harley to give us a peek at Unit Seventeen, we may yet salvage something from this mission." She shook her small fist in the air. "We'll find that girl no matter what it takes."

A bolt of lightning snaked out of the trees and struck the dark figure on Billie's left. Ropes of electricity swarmed over the black form, twisting and hissing like a pit of snakes.

The shadow man took a few steps across the ground, but with each step it seemed to sink further into the earth. Its long arms thrashed as it disappeared up to its knees. Then it was gone to its waist. Like a man sinking in quicksand, the shadow was slowly reduced to nothing. The lightning stopped.

Billie stared at the smoking patch of ground. Her red lips were open in a circle of surprise.

Harley Davisidaro stepped from the trees. "There's no need to go looking for me," she said. "I'm already here."

ELEVEN

There were two more of the shadowy forms in the woods behind Noah, but Harley ignored them. She kept the gun pointed straight at Billie.

The red-haired girl stared back at Harley. Billie might have been careful to hide her true feelings before, but now she was making no such effort. Her bright turquoise eyes held a mixture of surprise and rage.

"I see that Cain has given you one of his little toys," she snarled. "He and his pitiful band of misfits will never learn to keep out of other people's business."

Harley glanced over at Noah. "Are you all right?"

"Yeah." Noah nodded. "At least I think so." He took a step toward Harley. As he moved, the dark creatures at his back shifted to follow.

Harley waved the lightning pen toward them. "Stay back," she warned.

Billie peered past Harley into the woods. "Tell me, dear," she said sweetly. "Are you alone?"

"I've got all the help I need," said Harley. She aimed the weapon squarely between Billie's strange eyes.

The shorter girl seemed unconcerned by the little pen-shaped device. She stepped toward Harley. "You *are* alone," she said. A dark, twisted smile came over her face. "Cain has sent you to face me all on your own. How wonderful." She took another step forward.

"I will shoot," Harley warned.

Billie opened her eyes wide and pressed one hand against her forehead. "You'd hurt little me?"

"Don't let her get near you!" shouted Noah. He staggered over to Harley's side.

"I won't," said Harley. She kept her thumb resting lightly on the weapon's twin triggers. "I've got a pretty good idea what she's like."

"Noah has told me what happened to your father," said Billie. "Surely by now you must realize that you'll never find him on your own."

Harley shook her head. "I'll find him," she said firmly. But as the words came out of her mouth, she felt a wave of despair. She had made no progress so far. Maybe her father would be missing forever. Billie was right—it was hopeless.

"I can help you," said Billie. Her voice became a soft, comforting whisper. "I've got resources that Cain never dreamed of."

A ray of hope burst through Harley's gloom. "You do?"

Billie nodded. Her blue-green eyes were so bright, so understanding. She walked toward

Harley with her hand outstretched. "Why don't you give that thing to me?" she said. "Then we can go get your dad."

Harley lowered the weapon. It all seemed so right. Billie was the only hope she had of finding her father. Her only hope. She had to trust Billie.

Something struck Harley hard on the side, sending her staggering back into the trees. She raised her hand, jamming the lightning pen against the bare flesh at someone's neck. Only then did she realize it was Noah.

"Harley, don't!" he cried. "Don't listen to her. Don't look into her eyes."

For a moment Harley felt an overwhelming need to trust Billie. She would do anything for Billie. Then the feeling was gone.

"I'm okay," Harley said. Over Noah's shoulder, she saw the shadow men moving forward. "What do you think about running?"

Noah glanced over his shoulder. "Great plan."

Together Noah and Harley sprinted off between the thick trunks of the trees. Harley quickly drew several strides ahead. When she realized he was falling behind, she eased off and dropped back to Noah's side. "You sure you're not hurt?"

Noah nodded. "Not physically, anyway." He looked away. "Where are we going?"

"Back to the cabin," said Harley. "I left a motorcycle there."

It took ten minutes to reach the boulder field near the cabin. As they ran, clouds spread across the sky and sharp, cold breezes began to blow through the woods. From the heavy feeling in the air, Harley could tell that a storm was coming. She only hoped they could get to someplace warm and dry before it hit.

As they picked their way between the huge stones, Noah grabbed Harley by the sleeve and pulled her back into the shadow of a boulder. "Look," he whispered. He raised his hand and pointed up the slope.

Harley peeked around the side of the boulder. On the hill above, she could make out the gleam of the stolen motorcycle. Standing beside it was the black form of one of the shadow men.

"Oh, great." She drew back and slumped against the cold stone. "So much for getting out of here that way. Looks like we'll have to walk."

Noah leaned back beside Harley. He glanced at her for a moment and started to say something, then looked down at the ground. "I'm sorry," he mumbled.

Harley frowned. "Sorry about what?"

Noah's face blushed red. "I'll tell you later," he said.

For a moment Harley thought about pressing him, but she let it slide. She pointed down the hill toward the lake. "If we walk down there, we can probably get away without the shadow up on the road seeing us."

"Right," agreed Noah. He took one step away from the boulder, then spun around. "I've got an even better idea."

"What?"

To Harley's amazement, Noah actually smiled. "The boat," he said. "We can take the boat across the lake. Heck, we can take it all the way down to the state park at the other end. There's bound to be a phone we can get to and call Dee."

It certainly sounded better to Harley than walking or running to town. The adrenaline of her long ride back to Stone Harbor had long since started to fade. She was feeling so tired that she didn't want to take one step more than necessary. "Let's go for it," she said. "I've always liked boats."

"Now if we can just find the key," said Noah. He trotted away from the boulder and down the curving stone path toward the cabin.

Harley followed and caught up to him just as he slipped through the shattered door. "I hope you can find it in there," she said. "This place is a mess."

"You've been here?"

"About twenty minutes ago."

Noah turned to her and frowned. "How did you find us, anyway? Are you some great tracker, or did Cain tell you how to detect the implant in my shoulder?"

"Neither," said Harley. "I came down here and saw one of the shadow guys leaving. I followed it, and it led me to you. Very simple."

"I'm glad something is."

Harley followed Noah into the cabin. Broken glass crunched under her feet as she walked across the main room. The couch leaned against the back wall. Lamps, tables, and chairs were all smashed into kindling. "Wow. What happened here?"

Noah was searching in the kitchen for the boat key. "Billie and I were . . ." He paused for a second. "We were by the couch. Two of the shadow things broke in, and we had to run for it." He stopped again, and an angry scowl crossed his face. "I guess we didn't really have to run for it. Billie staged the attack."

"You couldn't have known that," said Harley. She looked at the couch leaning crazily against the wall of the cabin.

Harley could imagine just how "close" to that couch Noah and Billie had been. She could also imagine how close Billie had been to Noah. The image didn't thrill her one bit.

"Here it is!" Noah shouted from the kitchen. He ran over to her holding a chain of rattling keys. "Next stop, telephone."

They left the cabin and started down the hill to the lake shore. Hidden behind a screen of skinny young trees, a floating dock came in sight, along with a small shed.

"Where's the boat?" asked Harley.

"Over there." Noah pointed at a dark green tarpaulin spread over something on the ground. "You have to take them out of the water in the winter, just in case the lake freezes. Don't worry. It's aluminum. The two of us can carry it."

Quickly they pushed off the tarp. The boat was nothing fancy, just bare gray metal with a couple of bench seats. Together they carried it out to the end of the dock and dropped it into the water with a splash. Noah tied the little vessel to the end of the dock, then both of them hurried up the hill to the metal shed.

Noah sorted through the keys and opened the shed. The metal door opened with a squeal of rusty hinges. "You take this stuff down," he said, handing Harley an armload of paddles and life jackets. "I'll grab the motor."

Harley stumbled back to the dock under the weight of the gear. She dropped it into the boat and was just straightening up when she saw the dark shapes moving through the trees above. "Noah!" she shouted. "They're coming!"

Noah emerged from the shed with a boat motor cradled in his arms. It was small, but it was heavy enough that Noah descended the hill awkwardly.

Billie and a pair of the shadow men followed a

few paces behind him. "Well," the red-haired girl called down the slope. "This is very resourceful. Too bad you weren't a bit faster."

Harley took hold of the pen weapon and pointed it up the hill. "Don't come any closer," she said. To her surprise, Billie stopped.

Noah stepped past Harley and climbed into the boat with the motor still in his arms. "Thirty seconds," he whispered. "That's all I need." He began to clamp the motor onto the tail of the boat.

"You can still give up now," Billie called down the slope. "Throw the weapon in the water. It'll be much better for everyone."

Harley looked away from Billie. She didn't want to be caught again by the girl's power.

There was a soft noise from the water beside the dock. Harley glanced down and saw something small bobbing in the water. As she was trying to make it out, there was a soft plop as another object rose to the surface. It was a clear lump about the size of Harley's fist.

"Ice?" she wondered, puzzled.

"What?" Noah asked. He was still bent over the engine.

More ice rose to the surface. "There's ice in the water," said Harley.

"Maybe the lake is freezing?"

"From the bottom up?" Harley glanced back up the hill. Billie and the two shadows stood calmly.

"Hurry," Harley urged. "Something's not right."

"Everything's not right," said Noah. He sat up straight. "All right, let's just hope this sucker starts." He grabbed the starting rope and pulled. The first pull brought only a weak cough from the motor. With the second came a stuttering roar. Blue-white smoke billowed from the engine as it ran for a moment, then died.

Harley tightened her grip on the weapon, holding it toward Billie and the two shadows. She couldn't understand why they didn't approach.

Noah gave the starting rope a third try. This time the engine roared, stumbled, then settled into a soft popping rumble. "Come on," Noah called. "Let's get out of here."

Harley took a last look at the still figures up the hill, then turned to climb into the boat. As she did, the dock bumped up and down under their feet. She staggered and looked down. There were no waves, but the dock was moving. It bumped up and down again, shaking Harley so badly that she almost lost her footing.

"Get off of there!" Noah shouted. He stretched out his hand toward Harley.

She stepped toward the boat. Her hand was only inches from Noah's when the dock was flung from the water.

Harley pinwheeled into the air. As she spun over the lake she had a glimpse of another of the shadow men holding the dock above its head. A ring of ice floated around its dark form.

Then Harley hit the water and felt the shock of cold. Some of it might have come from the presence of the shadow, most because it was November, but whatever the reason, the water was just plain freezing.

The frigid water squeezed the air from Harley's lungs as she splashed into the lake. She was a good swimmer, but now her arms and legs only spasmed uncontrollably. The lightning pen slipped from her fingers. Her jeans and sweater were immediately soaked through, dragging her downward like a coat of bricks.

Murky green-gray water swirled around her, growing darker as she sank. In seconds her lungs were burning for air.

There was a loud splash from above her, and a dark form flashed down. Harley looked up toward the surface of the lake. Against the rippling silver of the water's surface she could see a black shape coming to finish her.

The light slipped away as she sank into the cold darkness.

TWELVE

Noah searched blindly though the dark water. The lake was at least twenty feet deep here, and silty enough that below ten feet the light was all but gone.

He was nearing his limit. Another five seconds and he would have to return to the surface for air. Thirty seconds after that, he would have to get out of the cold water or die from hypothermia.

He kicked downward, plunging toward the lake's muddy bottom. His hand touched something. At first he thought it was some kind of water grass. Then he realized it was the floating cloud of Harley's hair. A burst of adrenaline drove him downward another foot. His fingers moved down the side of her cold cheek and grasped the heavy leather coat. Harley's arms came up and the coat pulled free, leaving Noah holding a mass of wet leather. He pushed the coat away and grabbed for her again. This time his fingers caught in the sweater at her shoulder.

Harley was still sinking, drifting toward the black mud at the bottom of the lake. Now Noah was going with her. Holding on as hard as his half frozen fingers would allow, Noah pushed for the surface. The rate of their descent into the icy lake slowed and began to reverse itself. Noah's lungs burned as the light grew brighter with painful slowness.

Then the water dropped away. Noah opened his mouth and drew in cold, painful, glorious air. Kicking hard with his legs, he pulled Harley's head free of the water.

Her mouth and eyes were closed. Her legs and arms drifted limply in the water.

"Breathe!" Noah shouted into her face. "Breathe!"

Harley stirred weakly. Water trickled from the corner of her mouth.

Noah shivered violently. He had to get out of the water, and he had to do it now. He hooked his arm under Harley's chin and started stroking for the shore.

The thirty-foot trip seemed to grow longer as he swam. It stretched into a marathon of cold and fear. Finally Noah's feet felt the muddy bottom, and he dragged Harley up onto the shore. Her face had become a frightening blue-gray.

Billie and the shadow men were waiting. "Is she dead?" called the red-haired girl.

Noah didn't bother to reply. He leaned over Harley, turning her onto her side. More water poured from her lips. Her mouth dropped open.

But still she didn't breathe. Noah turned Harley onto her back and began compressing her sternum under his hands.

His Red Cross training was years in the past, and he feared that he had forgotten everything, but there was nothing else he could do besides try his best. He pumped Harley's chest five times, then leaned over and pressed his mouth over hers. Harley's lips were cold as he blew breath into her lungs. Her chest rose slightly, then fell.

Harley moaned.

Noah leaned away as Harley's neck jerked back. A flood of lake water spilled onto the muddy bank, and then Harley drew a long, wheezing breath.

Billie clapped her hands. "How wonderful," she said. "How valiant. I do believe that's the bravest thing I've ever seen." The mocking applause echoed over the still lake.

Noah glared at her. "Shut up," he said through gritted teeth. He got his hands under Harley's shoulders and helped her into a sitting position. "How do you feel?" he asked.

A tremble ran through Harley's body. "C-C-Cold," she stammered.

Now that the emergency was over, Noah also felt near freezing. The icy water had drawn all his strength, leaving him exhausted and shivering. He looked up at Billie without hope. "We need to get her warm."

To Noah's surprise, Billie nodded. "Of course," she said. "It wouldn't do to have either one of you dying now." She smiled. "You're worth much more alive."

The shadow man who had upset the dock emerged from the water, shedding ice with every step. The lake behind it was filled with floating chips and chunks, like a glass of iced tea. With Billie walking ahead, the three shadows escorted Noah and Harley up to the cabin.

Harley leaned against Noah as they walked. Her normally olive skin was still pale, and her steps were unsteady.

"Hold on," Noah said softly. "We'll get warm." He put his arm around Harley's thin waist and held her tight as they went up the trail and through the door of the cabin.

The splintered remains of the door served as firewood. The fire burned the old dry wood enthusiastically. Noah and Harley sat so close to the flames that steam rose from their wet clothing. For Noah, even that wasn't good enough. He wanted to crawl right into the fireplace and curl up in the embers until the heat burned out the ice that had gathered in his bones. It was an ice formed by more than cold water. What Billie had done was far colder than the lake.

Billie looked down at the two of them. "Watch them," she said to one of the shadows. "Don't let them move. Don't let them touch anything. Understand?"

"Yes," rumbled the shadow.

"I'm going to go and arrange our transportation," said Billie. "It's time we left this place." She walked out of the cabin, broken glass crunching like gravel under her feet.

Harley leaned against Noah's shoulder. "Thank you," she said.

"For what?" asked Noah.

"For saving me, of course." Harley trembled violently. "I didn't just think I was going to die. I was *sure* of it."

"Hey, you saved me from Billie about five minutes before," said Noah. "I'd say we're even."

"Maybe," said Harley. She turned her head and brought her face only an inch away from Noah's. "But I won't forget what you did for me."

Noah closed the distance between them, pressing his mouth hard against Harley's. This time her lips were not cold.

Bitter laughter came from the doorway. Noah pulled back from Harley and turned to see Billie standing in the doorway. "I should be hurt," she said. "After all we did together."

Noah felt himself flushing from both embarrassment and anger. "You forced me."

"Did I?" Billie asked. She walked across the room with an exaggerated bounce in her step. She leaned over Noah, bringing her turquoise eyes down close to his. "Was it so horrible?" she asked. "Did I really force you, or was it what you wanted?"

Noah felt a stab of guilt. He *had* been attracted to Billie. He would have liked to blame it all on Billie's power, but deep down he knew better.

I know the truth, said the cold voice in his mind. *You wanted me. You want me still.*

Noah shook his head. Billie's face would always be beautiful. But all Noah felt now was disgust. "Get away from me," he said flatly.

The red-haired girl laughed again. "Don't worry. You'll have plenty of time to get friendly with me again." She stood and walked across the room. "Everything is arranged," she said. "Our transportation will be here any moment." She pointed out the window. "Look!"

Noah followed the direction of her finger. Outside, the lake lay placid under a blue sky. He didn't see anything unusual at first. Then he spotted a black cloud rising over the trees on the other side of the water.

It was the wrong season of the year for thunderstorms, but this was obviously no ordinary cloud. It rose so quickly that Noah could see it grow, boiling upward into the cloudless sky.

Billie walked out the broken door. "Bring them," she called over her shoulder.

The shadow thing moved closer to Noah and Harley. "Come," said the creature in its deep voice.

"Our clothes are still wet," said Noah. "You make us go back out there now, and we'll freeze to death."

"Come," repeated the shadow. It moved closer. The chill breeze that poured from its body was far colder than anything Noah had felt in the lake.

"We're coming," he said. He climbed to his feet and stretched his hand down to Harley. "You think you can walk?"

"Yeah," Harley answered. "I think so." She reached up to take Noah's hand with her left, but as she rose her right hand reached into the fireplace and came out with a length of broken board. She swung past Noah, driving the sharp, flaming end of the wood into the chest of the dark creature.

The shadow turned translucent, like a statue made from smoky glass. Within its belly, the flames continued to lick upward.

"Run!" shouted Harley. She pulled her hand free from Noah's, ducked under the shadow's arm, and sprinted for the door.

Noah stood in shock for a moment, then darted after her. Harley led the way into the maze of boulders with Noah right behind. He followed as she dodged left, right, and left again.

"Where are you going?" he called.

"Away!" Harley shouted back. "We can figure out *where* later!" She looked back over her shoulder. With her black hair flying and her long legs pumping, she looked just the way she had when Noah first noticed her on the track at school. It had been only a few weeks ago, but it seemed to Noah as though it had been years.

Then a dark arm reached out and snagged Noah's shirt. He cried out in pain and fear as ice spread over his clothing.

Noah fell and tumbled against the base of a boulder. A sharp pain ran down his side as his ribs crashed into the stone. His head hit the hard ground with a solid thump, sending spots of white light rolling across his vision. There was a scuffling, thumping sound from up ahead, then a brief shout that had to be from Harley. Noah tried to rise. A wave of dizziness made him fall back.

By the time he was able to get to his feet, Billie and four of the shadow men were standing around him. Harley leaned warily against another of the boulders. From the icicles that dripped from her clothing, it was clear she'd had a run-in with one of the shadows, too.

"I see you two still haven't learned," said Billie. She folded her arms across her chest. "Let me make this very clear. I'd like to have the two of you alive. You, Noah, have some value to us—not much, but a little. However"—she pointed a finger at Harley—"Ms. Davisidaro is good for nothing but information. If I need to, I will personally grind her brain into a fine mash and extract that information by deciphering the RNA codes. Is that clear?"

Noah wasn't too certain he believed that Billie could do what she said, but her real message was clear enough. "We'll cooperate," he said.

"Now get down to the docks before I decide to take your heads and leave the rest of you behind," Billie ordered.

Noah and Harley were herded along between the shadows. As they walked down toward the water, Noah saw that the thunderhead building in the west had grown into a huge, towering anvil. Snakes of lightning slashed down among the trees on the opposite bank, and thunder rolled over the water. Bursts of cold wind made Noah shiver as they blew over his damp clothing.

Billie led the procession out to the end of the dock. The storm quickly grew closer. The clouds at its base rolled and heaved. As waves formed on the lake the dock began to rock up and down.

"Shouldn't we be looking for shelter?" asked Harley. "They may not teach you this down at superspy headquarters, but you're not supposed to hang around a lake during a thunderstorm."

"Be quiet," Billie ordered. "Watch."

Inside the twisting body of the storm, lights began to glow. Patches of red, green, blue, and yellow shone through the dark gray clouds. The lights began to circle. In the center, the clouds thickened and darkened. A handful of hailstones rattled down onto the dock and splashed into the water of the lake.

"Here comes our ride," said Billie.

From the center of the circling lights, a dark funnel stretched down to touch the earth. As it touched the surface of the lake, water began to move upward in a silver spiral. The funnel slowly approached the dock.

"You're going to kill us!" shouted Noah. "We can't ride in a tornado!" The wind grew stronger, tugging him toward the advancing funnel.

A dozen lightning bolts struck all at once, shearing limbs from nearby trees and blasting out pits in the ground. The clap of thunder was deafening. "We can, and we will!" Billie shouted over the fading rumbles. "Stand where you are!"

Another bolt of lightning struck. But this time it came not from the storm, but from up the hill.

The lightning sizzled into the shadow man nearest Harley. The thing writhed like a dying worm as it sank down to nothingness.

"Cain!" Harley shouted.

Noah looked up the hill and saw a figure running down the slope. In the glowing light of the storm, he could see only a dim shape, but the trench coat flapping in the wind was enough to identify the agent.

Another lightning bolt snapped from Cain's hands, blasting away one of the shadows on Noah's left. That left only one of the creatures standing between the two prisoners and the shore.

Harley broke from her position. She took two steps straight for the creature, then dodged left as neatly as any football halfback. "Noah!" she shouted as she reached the bank. "Come on! Hurry!"

Noah tensed and started to run.

"Noah," said Billie.

Her voice was soft, and it should have been lost in the growl of the nearing waterspout, but the sound of his name ran through Noah like a knife. He turned slowly and looked at Billie.

She stood at the very end of the dock with her arms stretched out toward him. *Love me,* said the voice in his head. *You and I are the same.*

The tornado was close behind her. It was larger than Noah had thought. The tip trailing into the lake was a good forty feet across. Strands of colored light ran through the funnel, swirling in a hypnotic dance.

Noah could feel Billie's power pulling at his mind. He took an unconscious step toward her.

"That's it," Billie coaxed. "Come with me."

The voice came both through his ears and through his mind. Billie's power pressed and tore, threatening to rip Noah free from all control of his own mind and body.

"No," he whispered. He shook his head. "No!" Inside Noah's mind something shifted, as though he'd just discovered a muscle he had never known before. With a single heave he pushed Billie from his skull. "I'm not going with you. It won't work anymore."

Billie's face twisted in a snarl as she lowered her arms. "You've seen only the beginning of what I can do." The tornado was almost on her. The water at her back was whipped into a frenzy.

"I've seen all I want," said Noah. He turned to go.

The shadow caught him with both hands.

Noah screamed as the dark creature lifted him from the ground. Infinite cold froze his lungs. His heart stopped in his chest.

Then the shadow man threw him into the center of the tornado.

EPILOGUE

Harley sat on the end of the dock.

With the passing of the storm, the wind had calmed. The temperature had returned to a brisk November chill. In her damp clothes, Harley was tempting pneumonia, but she no longer cared.

"I came as fast as I could," said Cain. The agent walked out onto the dock, his hard-soled shoes thumping hollowly on the boards. "Umbra put a trap in my path."

Harley turned her head and looked up at the tall man. "I don't blame you for not coming sooner," she said. "But I do blame you for sending me away."

Cain was silent, and most of his long face was hidden under the shadow of his hat, but Harley thought she could see pain in the set of his mouth.

"Why did you send me?" Harley asked. "The whole trip to New York was a fake. You already knew all about those buildings I visited. Even if you didn't, you could have done a better job of following those people than I did." She gave a bitter laugh. "If you hadn't come to get me, Braddock would probably be roasting me over a pit by now."

The agent shook his head. "Don't underestimate

181

yourself," he said. "You did your task well. Better than we had any right to expect."

"But the task was worthless," said Harley. "Why did you send me away?"

Cain looked away. "It was a test."

"A test?" Harley smashed her hand into the dock. "Noah is missing because of a *test?* That's some price to pay for a pop quiz."

"It was important that we know how you would behave when confronted with such work," said Cain. "It was necessary that we determine the depths of your motivation."

Harley shook her head. She wanted to laugh and to cry, and she wasn't sure which one to do first. "I'd do anything to get my father back. If you haven't figured that much out by now, then you're an idiot."

The agent nodded. "I suspected as much, but there are others who weren't so sure of you. They wanted confirmation of your commitment if you were to be considered for membership."

"I never asked to be a member of anything," said Harley. She stood up. "All I want is my father back, and Noah back. Then I want to be left alone."

"There's no such thing as being left alone," said Cain. "Either you act or you are acted on."

Now Harley did laugh. "That's a wonderful philosophy," she said. "What is this group of yours? The Zen police?"

Cain pulled another of the pen weapons from

his pocket and began to flip it back and forth between his fingers. Long seconds passed before he looked up.

"There are four groups," he said at last. "Four organizations holding the keys to a power that goes back almost five thousand years. Between them, they stand behind every government in the world. They pull the strings that make the rest of us dance."

"And your group is one of them?" asked Harley. "You're part of something like Legion or Unit Seventeen or Umbra? You can count me out of it, then."

"No." Cain flipped the little pen around again and dropped it back into his pocket. "We're a small organization, with only a few members. We watch the other groups and try to hold the balance."

"What balance?"

"The balance that prevents any one group from overwhelming the others."

"What would it matter?" asked Harley. "They all seem to be equally bad."

Cain nodded. "Yes," he said. "But without the others to hold them back, any one of them would become pure tyrants." He looked out across the surface of the lake. "No matter how terrible the world seems now, you can't imagine what it would be like if any of these groups gains complete control."

Harley thought for a moment. "So are you going to tell me what you know about my father?"

"Yes," said Cain. "If the rest of the organization agrees."

"And what about my mother?"

The agent shrugged his broad shoulders. "As I said, we're not sure if she *is* your mother. But we'll share what information we have if—"

"I know," Harley interrupted. "You'll share if you decide I'm good enough to be part of your little squad." She looked up into Cain's pale eyes. "If you want me in your group, it's going to take more than a lot of mystical crap. I've had it with all the mumbling and rumors. I want the truth, understand?"

Cain nodded. "I understand," he said. "But *you* have to understand how delicate our job really is. We have to keep each group in balance without giving any an advantage. Sometimes this means people have to be sacrificed. In this case, it may mean that your father and Noah have to pay the cost of keeping the world in one piece."

"To keep the balance," said Harley.

"That's right," the agent agreed. "Balance."

"Yeah, well, I have a better idea," said Harley.

"What?"

She walked past Cain, brushing against his trench coat as she stepped off the dock onto the shore. "I'm going to destroy them all," she said.

To be continued . . .